M

I was on the street, running, holding my side where blood dripped down. The bullet-headed man was behind me. I ran the five blocks to my office. When the lighted glass doors of our lobby were half a block away, I slowed to find my keys. The second man was there ahead. He had his knife. I ran again. I had less than ten steps on him at full speed. I had no time for keys. I pulled my head down and went through the glass side panels next to the doors in a shower of shattered glass.

I fell, came up, and ran up the stairs without looking back. I reached our floor, hit our door — and bounced off. I hit it again. And again. It ripped open and I fell inside. I stumbled into Delaney's private office, got the gun out of his drawer, sat in his chair, held the gun in both hands, aimed it at the open doors — waited.

Berkley Books by Mark Sadler

HERE TO DIE
MIRROR IMAGE
TOUCH OF DEATH

Here to Die

MARK SADLER

BERKLEY BOOKS, NEW YORK

HERE TO DIE

A Berkley Book / published by arrangement with
the author

PRINTING HISTORY
Random House edition published 1971
Berkley edition / April 1989

ISBN: 0-425-11535-6

A BERKLEY BOOK ® TM 757,375
Berkley Books are published by The Berkley Publishing Group,
200 Madison Avenue, New York, NY 10016.
The name "BERKLEY" and the "B" logo
are trademarks belonging to Berkley Publishing Corporation.

PRINTED IN THE UNITED STATES OF AMERICA

10 9 8 7 6 5 4 3 2 1

To John and Lori,
with presumption

Let there be no inscriptions upon my tomb, let no man write my epitaph. No man can write my epitaph. I am here to die . . . Let my character and motives repose in obscurity and peace, till other times and other men can do them justice.

—ROBERT EMMETT
September, 1803

Here to Die

1

FRANK CARLOS CALLED ME at 2:00 A.M. on a Sunday night in February. To be exact: 2:05 A.M. on Monday morning.

"Long distance for Mr. Paul Shaw."

There were long-distance noises. I had time to light a cigarette, and work up a small anger, before a man's voice came on the other end.

"Shaw? My name is Frank Carlos. You don't—"

I said, "I don't like calls at two A.M."

I heard him take a deep breath. "Sorry. I forgot the time difference. It's only eleven here. A few minutes after, I think. I . . . We're living in Malibu now . . . for a time . . . California. I . . . I've been waiting all weekend. Trying to decide if I should call you . . . or wait . . . or . . ."

He was talking it out, like a man who had been alone for some time with no one to talk to. Drinking. I could hear the liquor in his voice, and almost see his tense grip on the phone. His voice had a faint accent I knew: Spanish, overlaid with New York slum and Harlem hip. Only a residue under well-educated American. A Puerto Rican voice that had climbed far out of East Harlem.

"We've got a Los Angeles office, Mr. Carlos," I said. (*Thayer, Shaw and Delaney—Security and Investigations*, New York and Los Angeles. Delaney was our L.A. man, let him lose sleep.)

A silence. Then, "I don't know about your office. I found

your number in Judy's old address book. I need help, Shaw."

The bell tolled distant out of my past. Maureen, my wife, shifted in bed beside me, mumbled through wisps of thick red hair as if she could hear my thoughts. *Judy.* Judith Tower. She *had* married a man named Carlos. Six years ago. It was my turn to grip the telephone hard.

"Something about Judy?" I asked.

"Maybe she's only left me, Shaw. Maybe she's just on a fling," Frank Carlos' voice said from the far end. "It's been two weeks without a word. Not even a postcard. Judy wouldn't do that, Shaw, I know—"

"Have you reported it to the police?"

"No!" He bit the word off. He had a tight hold on himself despite his slurring. "If she's just left me, I don't want the cops on her back, or on mine."

"You think she's left you? You've said it twice."

Another silence, as if he was looking around that room out in Malibu for an answer. "I thought she had at first, yes. Now I don't know. You know her, Shaw. Would she leave me without telling me to my face? Two weeks without even a call? That's not Judy. I thought . . . you know how to find people . . . you—"

"How have you looked for her so far?"

His voice didn't rise; it went down, flat and cool. "Shaw, no one's seen Judy for two weeks. If you come out, I'll give you the details. If you don't come, the details don't matter, do they? Come to 112 Torino Canyon, Malibu." He hung up.

I lay back on the pillows. Maureen moved against me in the bed. I went out into the living room. Through our big window the park was white with last week's snow, the bare trees black in the night. From our penthouse I could see the park and the city up into Harlem. The penthouse Maureen's success in the theater paid for, and the city we had all been going to conquer ten years ago. Maureen had done it, and in a way, so had I. But Judy?

Six years since I had heard her voice, Judy's. That, too, had been a telephone call.

2 ⌒

Her voice a whisper from the dark. "Paul? Darling? I miss you. Oh, I miss you."

I felt the hollow ache inside. The loss of a man's first real love is like no loss he will ever have again.

"Judy? Where the hell are you? It's four A.M."

Soft from the phone, "I know. I miss you, Paul. I had to tell you, talk to you."

"After two years? Where are you?"

I heard my own voice in the shabby cold-water apartment, and remembered Maureen beside me. For an instant, hearing Judy's voice, I had forgotten my wife. Forgotten I had been married two years, Judy the past.

"I don't want to talk, Judy," I said.

"I know," she said. "I'm on the Coast. Can you hear the sea? It's dark, just the moonlight out there on the sea." She stopped; then, "Paul? I'm married. Tonight. I got married today, and I miss you. I had to tell you, talk to you."

No matter how real and solid a man's new life is, he never really gives up a last small hope that he and his first love can, someday, somewhere, exist again. Until now only I had married.

"Tonight?" I said. "And you call me? Swell! Who's the lucky man?"

"You don't know him. Frank Carlos, an actor, playwright. It

doesn't matter, Paul, I don't want to talk about Frank. I want to tell you I miss you. I'll always miss you, Paul."

Two years we'd had, off and on, Judy and I, and she had always talked as if she lived a separate life with each person she knew. One person did not affect the other. If she had just left another man's bed to come to me, the other man no longer existed once she was with me. No connection at all.

"What am I supposed to say, Judy?"

"Nothing," she said. "Just listen. Tomorrow I'll be a good wife. Tonight I miss you. I just wanted you to know. I want you to know I'll always miss you, darling, and maybe I want you to miss me sometimes."

I heard her voice in the cold, cheap apartment long after she had hung up. In California, in a honeymoon hotel at the edge of the Pacific, with a new husband, but her mind alone and back in the past of New York streets with me. Judy.

3

"Missing?" Maureen said. "Judy? Her husband called you?"

"Two weeks without a word. He wants me to look."

I had my bag packed—spring clothes and a topcoat: it's not that warm in California on February nights. Maureen is a small girl, just like Judy, but her long hair is red, not dark, and she is prettier, and she can use and control her high talent as Judy never could. The difference between Maureen's great success and Judy's relative failure—control.

Maureen watched me pack my shoulder holster and

working pistol: a light Colt Agent with a two-inch barrel, six shot.

"Is she in trouble, Paul? Danger?"

"Frank Carlos sounds worried."

"Then you have to go, don't you?"

I closed my bag. "You're sure, baby? It is Judy. I can give it to Delaney, Thayer wants me to. I've got work here, and Thayer's pretty mad about me going out there."

"No, you have to go. I don't think I'd like it if you'd forgotten Judy completely, Paul. I'll keep busy."

The penthouse glowed with cold winter sun when I left. So did Maureen. I felt like a man going back in time, losing some of the present. A sense of returning to the unfinished. I held Maureen tight when I kissed her.

As I drove out to Kennedy International, I thought again of that last time Judy had called. On her wedding night. To say she missed me. That was Judy. To feel was to act. To think was to say—without guilt, or fear, or calculation. From the very beginning, that had been Judy. The beginning . . .

. . . *A crowded party, and someone played the piano. Some show tune the glittering crowd wanted, a current hit. In a black sweater and black pants I felt like a poet among peacocks.*

She sat before me on the floor, small and pretty, very young, with dark hair. "I'm Judy Tower. I've watched you in classes. You're not good, but you could be with work."

"Paul Shaw," I said. "I think you're very good."

"I know I am," she said. "There's not a real actor here, you know? Can we go somewhere, Paul? Talk?"

Her date was another young actor—Rick Elliot. A little older than I, maybe twenty-two, blond and handsome and on his way up. She was sorry, she told Elliot, but she was leaving with me. Elliot was angry. I balanced on the balls of my feet, felt masculine. We went to a bar. We walked up Eighth Avenue. She really wanted to talk. We walked, and talked, for hours, and in those hours I stopped feeling masculine and fell in love. Later, she told me she had wanted me for weeks.

"When I don't want you," she said, "I'll tell you."

"Unless I tell you first."

"Yes. No lies, no faking. Maybe we'll last forever, Paul."

It saved money to live together in her place. We kept our money jobs to pay for classes. In our scene work we slashed at each other because that was the only way to learn. We thought only of learning, and of each other. Judy and I.

4

OUR LOS ANGELES OFFICE is off Wilshire Boulevard in Hollywood. Hollywood, because our work has a way of focusing on the tight whirl of an affluent upper middle class that lives on high cliffs at the edge of its income. A nervous world of sudden change, desperate "fun," and despair tomorrow. People who never looked to find what they wanted to do, but only what they could do to make the most money the fastest, glitter the most. A world not of accomplishment and pride, but of position and reward—Acapulco every month; Europe every year. At least.

Dick Delaney was out running the check on Frank Carlos I had called ahead to ask for. I took an inconspicuous blue company Plymouth and headed for the Santa Monica Freeway. Coming to Los Angeles in February is unreal, like passing through snow mountains into a remote valley where it is always summer. On the Freeway the traffic moved locked together like a river in a narrow canyon, massive in its weight and speed.

At the sea, and Santa Monica Pier, everything slowed, and I blended into the coast highway going north. The sea, and the endless beaches and bikinis, passed for twenty minutes to the left. Then the sea vanished, and Malibu began— one solid row of houses between the highway and the beach. Backed against the road for miles, the narrow strip of houses gave few glimpses of the sea. It was like running along behind ranks of silent people with their backs turned to you, oblivious to your existence. The sea fenced off, stolen.

I found Torino Canyon, turned off up into the hills, and the houses became steadily smaller, the road more broken. It wound on through the dry brown hills, dotted like African *veldt* with the dusty green of twisted live oaks. I watched the side dirt roads, the numbers becoming lower the farther I went from the sea, the countryside growing more rustic. Frank Carlos was not living in the high-income area.

I saw the man out of the corner of my eye, and hit my brake. He came out of the dry brush at the edge of the road. He stopped a few feet out into the road, and waited for me to pass—arrogant and bored with my interruption. A broad, muscular, long-haired young man in faded Levis and a gray work shirt. His sharp face stared off into space, uninterested in me. I passed, and he crossed the road behind me to a yellow sports car parked in the bushes.

I looked back at the road just in time to glimpse a rural mailbox stenciled: Johnson, 112 Torino Canyon. Above the stenciled name was a hand-lettered sign: Carlos. I turned into the dirt road that led upward from the mailbox. In my rear-view mirror I saw the young man at the yellow sports car staring after me, alert. I stopped inside the dirt road. Before I could get out, the long-haired youth was in the car, made a hard U-turn, and went off in a cloud of dust.

He had been uninterested in me—until I had turned into the road to where Frank Carlos lived. I drove up the side road.

The house at the end was small, half covered by a brilliant red bougainvillaea. A gray VW stood under a canvas shelter that had space for two cars. The hills rose steeply and shadowed the silent house. Too silent, the house, with the VW still here. Not even a bird called. I had left my gun in my bag at the office. I found a two-by-four, and went inside.

The small house was littered with the remains of solitary living by an un-domestic man: bottles of tequila, squeezed lemons, a carton of salt. And the man himself.

He lay on his back in a pool of dried blood.

His eyes were closed, his brown face pale, and his one arm flung out toward the telephone table near him. I knelt down over him.

He was alive.

Shallow breathing, a weak pulse, but his heart beat under his bloody shirt. About six-feet-three, slender, but his legs were muscled in ragged denim shorts. A strong face, not handsome, with a large nose, and eyes with a faintly oriental cast, like most Puerto Ricans. The skin of his face was scarred and pitted, his black hair was cut short, and he had a mustache that drooped thick. I had little doubt he was Frank Carlos.

He had been stabbed, but there was a heavy pistol under the telephone table. The wounds in his left shoulder and arm had already dried. They weren't the major wound. His right hand rested on a thick cloth pressed to his side. The cloth was matted with dried blood. Before he had lost consciousness, he had stopped the heaviest flow of blood with the cloth. It had saved his life. A tough man.

I found a pencil, picked up the gun by the barrel. An S & W Highway Patrolman, it had been fired twice. I put it back. I thought about the young man in the yellow sports car. But Frank Carlos, if it was him, had been stabbed hours ago. Early this morning.

I stood up. There was only one thing on my mind—Judy. Missing wife, the husband calls for a detective to find her, and then someone tries to murder the husband. What did I tell the police? How did I play it? I knew what John Thayer, my ice-water senior partner, would say—give it to the police. But where did Judy fit, where was she, why was she missing? I knew what the police would think, and how they would handle her, but the wounded man had to have help.

I called the police.

Then I searched the small house. There wasn't much to search. I found a framed picture of the wounded man and Judy. So he was Frank Carlos. It was clear that he and Judy were only living here temporarily, their suitcases still partly packed. I didn't think any of Judy's clothes were missing— there were four large suitcases of her clothes, and the closet was full. I found one address book, new and almost empty. It had Frank Carlos' name in it. A fresh, new book, as if starting a new life. Judy's thick address book that I remembered well wasn't there. Like most young actresses, she always carried it with her. I took the new address book.

From the papers on the desk in the living room, Frank Carlos was working on a play of his own. There were also work sheets for some kind of play at something called The Theater of Elemental Force. That was all, and I checked Carlos. He was still breathing, but slowly, in shock. The last thing I found, as the sirens of the police finally began to wail up from Malibu, were two bullet holes close together in the wall. Frank Carlos had shot at his attackers, but had missed.

Three police cars and an ambulance poured into the yard outside, like an invasion force. They came in with their hands resting on their pistols in side holsters. From the Sheriff's Office. They paid no attention to me at first. One stood near me, while the others went to work on the room, the bushes outside, the gray VW, and the dirt road. A doctor worked on Carlos.

After some ten minutes a short man in civilian clothes approached the doctor. "How long, Doc?"

"Seven or eight hours. Lost a lot of blood. Three stab wounds, some big knife. I'll get him to the hospital now."

"No bullet wounds?" the civilian asked.

"No," the coroner said. He waved to his ambulance crew. They carried Frank Carlos out on a stretcher.

The civilian turned to me. "I'm Captain Watts, Malibu station. Who are you?"

"Paul Shaw, a friend. I just came in, and—"

"Friend of Frank Carlos? Seen the wife?"

"No," I said. "You know Carlos, Captain?"

"We've been keeping an eye on him since he got out of jail, yeh," Captain Watts said.

"Jail?" I said.

"You don't know much, for a friend," the captain said.

"No, I'm an old friend of Judy Carlos'," I said.

"The wife, huh? She's white, isn't she?"

"Is that important?"

"I've seen a lot of white–Mex trouble in my day, Shaw."

"Frank Carlos is Puerto Rican."

"Same thing," Watts said. "Where you a friend from?"

"New York," I said. "We've got an L.A. office." I showed him my license.

His eyes flattened. "Private dick? Why didn't you say so? What brought you?"

I made up my mind right then. Judy was mine. If she was in trouble, no matter what she had done, I would find her. I wasn't going to leave her to a sheriff's man who didn't like Frank Carlos or white–Mex "trouble."

"I'm in L.A. on other work," I said. "Judy Carlos is an old, good friend. I came to call, that's all."

I told him I'd been in New York, or on a jet, when Frank Carlos had been stabbed, and he lost interest in me. That was the way I wanted it. He wouldn't have told me anything anyway.

He let me go, after getting a statement of how I'd found the wounded Carlos, and I went to my car. Frank Carlos wasn't going to talk for some time—if the police would let me near him at all. I had nothing to go on. But I was supposed to be a detective, and I wanted to find Judy very much now.

5

I SAT WITH DICK DELANEY in our office.

"He got out of jail recently," I said. "That should make him easy to check out."

Delaney is the perfect man for us in the world of Southern California. Tough, graying, and tanned, he passes for one of the handsome affluent, while inside he has the steel mind of a New England farmer. He lives on a small ranch in the hills, has mastered the art of not drinking at wild parties while seeming convivial, and is as thorough as an accountant.

"He was easy anyway," Delaney said. "He got out one month ago, I could have told you. What do you know about him, Paul?"

"He married an old friend. What should I know?"

"That depends. He's something of a celebrity in a couple of ways. You don't follow sports?"

"Not much. Start at the beginning, Dick."

He swiveled in his desk chair, held a typed report, but didn't read it. He didn't have to. "He's half Puerto Rican, the better half. His mother was Irish, deserted when Frank was seven. A juvenile arrest got him a term in a correctional school. That school had someone who knew a lot, because after that it was college for Carlos, basketball, track, and his M.A. from San Perdido State College. An injury turned him to teaching. Then a one-shot role in a Hollywood movie that wanted his athletic name seems to have given him the theater bug."

"So that's where he met Judy," I said.

"Yeh. He studied acting, got some parts in small plays, started writing plays, and married Judith Tower six years ago. Some critics liked the plays, but there was no money in them, I guess, and no more movie parts. He'd been studying for his Ph.D. the whole time. Two years ago he became a professor of drama at San Perdido State, and assistant basketball coach."

I waited, but Delaney didn't go on. He laid down the typed report. The afternoon sun was hot through the windows.

"Well," I said. "What did he do, fix some games?"

"He led a strike of militants and protesters at San Perdido State. A year ago. It went on for forty days, closed the college. Police, the Guard, tear gas, TV, headlines, the whole works. Almost as big as San Francisco State."

I remembered. *That* Frank Carlos. "He went to jail for leading the strike?"

"He did. Two years, one suspended as a first offense. He had a clean record except for that juvenile arrest in East Harlem. No militant ties before the strike. Sort of emerged from nowhere. Did eight months, is on parole now."

"So he can't charge around after Judy, and if he called the cops, the newspapers'd have a field day," I said.

"I suppose that's why he called you in," Delaney said.

"Just what happened at San Perdido State?"

"Do you know the town, or the college?"

"The city some, not the school," I said.

Delaney considered. "They're a lot the same. A hamburger city, blue-collar, run by the Chamber of Commerce and the Lions Club. White power. A medium-sized black and Mexican ghetto under good control. The campus is an overgrown city college. Most students were local, apathetic, oriented toward education for a job. A small minority enrollment. Not much militant leadership. Black Student Union small and muddled, a tiny Black Panther chapter in the ghetto, a weak S.D.S. The only real leader on campus was Dave Eigen of S.D.S., but he was alone."

"You think they just used Frank Carlos? Conned him?"

"Could be. He rallied the uncommitted students all right. The trigger was paving a field for a parking lot. The Biology Department had a contract from the military, were adding staff. It just happened that the field was used by ghetto kids for baseball. The campus exploded—callous authority; bad priorities; insensitive to community needs; education serving the military. You know how it goes, Paul. A spontaneous explosion, the militants weren't ready. No focus for the majority. The strike sputtered for three days, and Frank Carlos took over. His popularity committed all the kids, made it big."

"Why did it fail after forty days?"

"Carlos got the students, but not the ghetto. No community support. Afraid or apathetic, who knows?"

Who did know about a ghetto? Fear, and apathy, they both stalk ghettos. Afraid and hopeless. But my mind wasn't on ghettos just now. It was on a name: Dave Eigen. I opened the new address book I'd found in the small house.

"It's a new address book, Dick," I said. "Only four entries besides obvious business addresses. As if Carlos had cleaned the deck after prison. One name is David Eigen."

"The S.D.S. leader," Delaney said. "So he's still in contact with Eigen? What're the other names?"

"Dr. Jonas Eyk, John Morgan, and The Carleton Club. Dr. Eyk and Morgan have San Perdido addresses. The club is L.A."

Delaney nodded. "I don't know Eyk, but John Morgan is the Black Panther captain in San Perdido."

I chewed on the possibilities. Frank Carlos had led a big militant strike. One month out of jail his wife vanished and he was almost killed. He'd started a new address book, but two of the three names in it were still militant leaders.

"Call the hospital, Dick," I said. "See if you can talk to Frank Carlos. Make an excuse, we're not in the case."

He made the call. I walked to the windows. The constant thick haze hung over Los Angeles. Carlos had gotten out of prison only one month ago. Which meant that Judy had vanished only two weeks after he came home. I didn't like the implications. Eight months alone, and gone in two weeks. Delaney hung up behind me.

"Carlos is still unconscious. No visitors. The police have him under guard. No comment."

"Give me a case, Dick. Something to cover me."

"The best'd be the Hammond divorce. He's a playboy, gets around a lot. You're looking for witnesses. You're going on?"

I nodded. "You better alert our lawyers."

"Lying to the police, it could cost your license."

"I'll try to be careful," I said. "What did you dig up on Judy Carlos? Any personal trouble?"

"Nothing public. The only mention of her was some small movie and theater parts. Critics say she's good."

"She is," I said, "but she's hard to work with, too honest."

"A man?" Delaney said. "Alone eight months."

"With Judy it could always be a man," I said. "The only thing it couldn't be is money. She never cared about money. When the rubber hits the road, money doesn't influence her. She always took the play she wanted, not the one that paid. It's one reason she never has made a name."

"A dreamer, Paul?"

"In a way," I said. "What's The Theater of Elemental Force, Dick?"

"Don't know, but I'll find out." He flipped on the intercom, gave his instructions, sat back. "You said The Carleton Club was in Carlos' address book?"

I checked it. "Yes, just the club, no name."

"It's a nice place near here. Run by Emil Tarra, an old racketeer, Paul. Not much record, but he skates thin. The place is a club-restaurant, not all its patrons are nice."

I stood up. "Okay, it's a start. Keep checking on Frank Carlos, Dick, and get me a motel room. Call Maureen, okay?"

"Sure, Paul." His phone rang. He listened, hung up. "That Elemental Force Theater is a far-out operation run by some nut named Max Alfreda. My girl's got the address if you want it."

"I want it," I said.

Ten years rolled away again as I walked out and took the address from the secretary. I remembered Max Alfreda.

6 🕊

He called two weeks after Judy and I moved together. He wanted to have lunch, talk to me.

"I am Max Alfreda."

A small, heavy man with a high shoulder and short leg that made him limp. The gaunt, handsome, ascetic face of a dark prophet. Genius or madman, no one was sure, and he would work with no one else on his productions. Judy had worked with him, under him, and could talk about him for hours—the poète maudit, *the theater of the future. In ten years he had finished only scenes and fragments. It was there in his face—hypnotic eyes, a sensual mouth, lines of strain.*

"You are in the theater?" he asked me. "You act?"

"I try."

"Try? For what? You do not try theater, you are theater! Theater is magic. How do you try magic, write magic, direct magic? Disorder! Learn the disorder of your body and mind. You agree?"

"I don't know," I said.

The glitter faded from his deep eyes. I realized what his face made me think of—the faces of those American Indian chiefs who fought the last futile battles against the inexorable white advance. A picture of Crazy Horse I had seen once, with that mixture of gentleness and fanaticism that can only suffer.

"Judith knows," he said, his eyes fixed on my face.

"What about Judy?"

His eyes were quite calm. "You are a young man. Therefore, you will have her the four days. I will have her only Tuesdays, Thursdays, and Saturdays. She lives with me those days, agreed?"

I didn't swear at him, or laugh at him. To make such a suggestion, he must have been her lover in the past, and he had to know he had lost her. I was the winner—now for sure. When I told her what Alfreda had said, I waited for her anger.

She smiled. "He's so vulnerable to the world, Paul."

Sad, not angry. Alfreda's desperate offer wasn't an insult, only a sign of his need of her. Her eyes soft behind her glasses.

"He's a genius, Paul, wonderful and exciting. He loves me in his way. But I don't want him, I want you."

I'd won, but I was uneasy. She hadn't thought his plan to share her was degrading, she had thought it only natural and very honest. Alfreda had known that. I began to sense that Judy could only be known by the guts, not the brain. She was beyond rational understanding. Max Alfreda knew her better than I did.

7 〜

THE THEATER OF ELEMENTAL FORCE was in a big, old mansion set back from a side street between Santa Monica and Westwood Village. The grounds were green in February and well kept, and a side yard had been made a parking lot. There were three cars in the lot: a Cadillac with a Pasadena license holder; an old Porsche from Los Angeles; and a battered 1960 Chevy wagon with no license holder. I parked next to the Porsche.

The mansion doors were open, and I walked into a bare foyer. On the left was an enormous room filled with rows of chairs. Made by tearing down walls between normal rooms, the big room filled the entire left side of the mansion. Platforms were set at various levels in the open center. Theater-in-the-round.

There were voices behind closed doors on the right. They stopped when I opened the doors. What had been the mansion library was deep in afternoon shadow. A long, high room, with heavy old-wood furniture, like a medieval hall. At the far end three men sat around a desk deep in shadow, silent and remote, for an instant like a distant tableau from the Dark Ages. Faces heavy with shadow, chiaroscuro, only dimly seen, and one seemed hooded, shapeless, with a high pointed head and no face.

Two of them stood up. Quickly, a chair scraping harsh. One stepped out at me. Not toward me, *at* me. He came into the muted light. A small black man with narrow hips, wide shoulders, and no eyes. Black reflecting circles instead of eyes. Dark glasses.

"You want something, man?" he said, and said over his shoulder behind him, "Mr. Max?"

Someone spoke from the rear, "I expect no one, Peter."

"Yeh," dark-glasses said. "Say your piece, man."

He wasn't black, no, the color of sand. But a "black" man because he wanted to be, with a thick shock of Afro hair. He wore a black leather jacket, a black beret, and I knew him.

"Pete?" I said. "Pete Wallace?"

. . . Judy wasn't alone at the bar table when I came in. A redheaded girl with her, Maureen, and Pete Wallace.

I faced only Judy. "What happened?"

"The season is mine, if I want it," she said.

Maureen tried not to watch us. Pete Wallace smiled. He always smiled. What the hell did the boy have to smile about? A scrawny mongrel out of an alley. Kicked through his seventeen years, yet smiling and eager to be someone. We all needed to be someone, to have someone.

I said, "Get some beers, Pete, okay?"

Judy said, "I have to take the work, Paul. I have to."

I had to look somewhere, so I looked at Pete Wallace going to the bar. He had the grace of a young cat. Being outside looking in kept a man lean—wits and hard work to survive. But where had he found the need to act when he had no chance? Alone since ten, Negro on top of it, and no chance.

"Don't, Judy," I said. "It's all summer. I can't go."

"Please, Paul, you know I'll go."

I knew she would go. Pete Wallace brought the beers . . .

Now, his eyes hidden behind the dark glasses, Pete Wallace leaned toward me—smooth and deliberate. No longer a boy.

"Well, damn, Paul! Where you been, man?"

"Still in New York, Pete."

The man who had remained seated at the far end of the dim room now stood and limped toward us. "Judy's Paul?"

No surprise. Time and space meant nothing to Max Alfreda. His vision was always the same, so what was time? He wore a brown monk's robe with the high pointed hood up around his Indian face. Still handsome with the fire inside, the same lines of suffering from a world that would not listen to him.

"I do not see your name," he said. "You are not working?"

Working had only one meaning for Max Alfreda—theater. What other work was there? What other universe?

"I gave it up a long time ago, Alfreda," I said.

"Gave it up?" An impossibility. "But Judy is with you again? She has not been to rehearsals in . . . in . . ."

"Two weeks, Mr. Max," Pete Wallace said gently.

"Yes, two weeks. What am I to do without Judith?"

"You last saw her two weeks ago?" I said.

"She does not even call me, no," Max Alfreda said.

"She hasn't called anyone," I said. "Frank Carlos hired me to find her. I'm a private detective now."

The third man moved from the desk in the rear, came out into the dim room. He looked at me, and at his watch. "I'm in a hurry, Alfreda. Is he staying long?"

He was a big, solid man in his late forties. His gray flannel suit was part solid businessman, part flamboyant country club. His car had to be the Cadillac. His face had the pink texture of health-club care, and his large hands were fleshy. His dark hair was handsomely gray, his mouth sensual and arrogant at the same time. Pete Wallace looked at him.

"You always in a hurry, man. Going to run right out of yourself someday," Pete said, and grinned at me. "Mr. Keating there, he's a rich man, you know, only he got real heart. He gives Mr. Max money, the big angel, even if what Mr. Max does is gonna bury Keating and all he got. How you figure that? I mean, he got money for Mr. Max right now."

Keating glared at Pete. "I like Alfreda's work."

"Good!" Alfreda said. "Listen to your body, Mr. Keating, your organs. Bathe in them. Act with irrationality, destroy your own world to purify it. Good!"

Keating said, "I expect to get what I'm paying for."

"Cool it, man," Pete Wallace said. "You way uptight. Nobody says you got to come around here. You go on back to your nice honky world if you want."

Max Alfreda said quickly, "He is here to help, Peter."

"Okay, Mr. Max, we let the man help. Only he don't tell us what to do, right?" Pete said. "Take the man's money, Mr. Max."

Max Alfreda nodded, then took Keating back to the desk in the shadows of the long room. In his monk's robe Alfreda looked like some militant priest leading a heretic to the dungeon. At the desk, Keating talked low, and began to write a check.

Pete Wallace watched the two of them. "He even looks like a pig, right?" Pete said. "Buyin' and sellin' with his honky money. Blood money, Paul, believe me."

"Where have you been all these years, Pete? Acting?"

"You know better." He smiled behind those dark glasses. "Just around. Around and learning. Took a small rap, and learned the way it really is inside. So when I got out, I went home to San Perdido and joined the fight, right?"

"The Black Panthers?" I said.

"Yeh, man. Fight force with force. Only way to get out from under Mr. Charlie's monkey." He grinned. "Only us actors never give up, right? Started a little theater in the ghetto up there. Who shows up to work with us—Judy! We had some good shows, man. Then the strike. Sort of fell apart after that."

"Where does Alfreda fit in, Pete?"

"Mr. Max got an idea to use the Panthers in a show, you know? Him and Judy come up to look us over, so I joined up. My kind of theater what Mr. Max is tryin'. Use all the violence, drag through the blood, come out clean."

Keating and Max Alfreda had returned from the rear of

the room while Pete Wallace was talking. Alfreda listened with nods of approval. Keating had the look of a man in a hurry to leave, but he didn't leave at once.

"Well," Keating said, "that's it then. All set."

Pete grinned. "The world of art thanks you."

Keating looked at me. "Can I give you a lift? Mr.—?"

"Paul Shaw," I said. "I've got my car."

"I got my own wheels too," Pete said. "So long, man."

I watched Keating go. He was far from the kind of man I would have expected to be the angel of an experimental theater.

"He comes around here a lot?" I asked Alfreda.

"No, not often."

"Max's biggest angel," Pete Wallace said. "More bread than he can use, maybe. Maybe he wanted to act when he was a kid."

"Does he know Judy?" I asked.

"No," Max Alfreda said. "Where is she, Judith? I cannot go on in this without her."

"You're working with the Black Panthers?"

Alfreda's eyes were alive. "The perfect vehicle for my work. Violence, cruelty, hate on the stage as it must be. Descend to purify. Elemental—no realism, no thought, no characters, no text to chain the organs. The disorder of our souls is in the battle of Panthers and society. Judith and I."

His fanatic eyes saw his vision in the shadows of the long room. His mind alone with his ideas.

"Where would she go, Alfreda?" I said.

"Go?" His mind came back slowly. "How can I know?"

Pete Wallace said, "A month I don't see her, man."

"Was her work here going well?"

Alfreda sighed. "Our work is not simple. No words written, we must draw from inside, slowly. After the husband came home, it was not good, no."

"He interfered?" I said. "Opposed you? Jealous?"

"No," Alfreda said, considered. "She was not happy. I

think she was close to the husband, in theater they are together. Between them comes something. The politics, perhaps. They are not as she wishes them to be. She does not concentrate."

"Neither of you has heard from her in two weeks?"

They both shook their heads.

"Where did she go from here the last time?"

"To her job," Alfreda said. "A waste of her time."

"The Carleton Club?"

"That is the place. She goes, she does not come to me the next day. Two weeks she does not come."

"All right," I said. "Thanks, Alfreda."

Pete Wallace said, "I'll walk out too."

We went to the door of the long room. It was evening now, the room all in shadow. I looked back, but Max Alfreda had already forgotten us. He was at his desk again, bent over in his monk's robe like some dark apparition from the Inquisition.

In the parking lot, Pete Wallace stopped me.

"Judy's really missing, man? I mean, is it bad?"

"It could be," I said.

"You trust that Frank Carlos?"

"Shouldn't I? Don't the Panthers trust him?" I didn't tell him about Frank Carlos. It could scare him off.

"Depends," he said. He looked off into space behind those dark glasses. "Maybe it don't mean beans, but Judy said something a couple of months ago. Carlos was in jail, right?"

"Something about a man, Pete?"

"You know Judy." He shrugged. "Some cat she was seein'. No name." He thought behind those dark glasses. "I don't see no trouble in San Perdido, only Carlos didn't make all friends."

"Any names of his enemies?"

"Who knows names? The mothers come out of the

bushes," he said, and then smiled. "Hey, Paul, a long time, right?"

"A long time," I said. "We both flopped."

"Yeh," he said. "Look, I'll nose around some in Perdido."

"My office is in the phone book. Any time, Pete, okay?"

"Check. My place in Perdido is 740 Fremont Street."

He got into the battered 1960 Chevy wagon. He still moved with that catlike grace, all muscles under his small exterior. When he drove out past me, the dark glasses still hiding his eyes, his face was set cold against the world. He could smile with a few whites, with me one of them, I hoped, but the rest were Mr. Charlie. What else had we given him?

As I drove away behind Pete, I heard an eerie wailing from inside the theater. Max Alfreda was working in his twilight world between genius and insanity.

8

I DROVE THROUGH BEVERLY HILLS among the aloof green castles of the movie industry. You can tell the god of a society, the power, by the label public relations men give to what they want to make important. Once it was the "art of auto making," then the "science of retailing," and now the "theater industry." Everything's an industry today. They stopped short of the "prostitution industry," but not by much.

The Carleton Club was less than five blocks from our office. A white building decorated with tubs of evergreen shrubs, and set in tree-lined parking lots full now with the cocktail-hour stampede. A running attendant took my low-income Plymouth with some distaste. I pretended not to hear the rubber burn on my wheels as I went inside. Everything was speed here.

Inside, it was an elegant speed. In dim, windowless light, bartenders moved behind the leather-padded bar with the precision of a Prussian drill regiment. Waiters flowed among the small tables of the cocktail lounge. The polished patrons gleamed like waxed furniture, their bodies and eyes in languid positions of ease and privilege, but their hands and mouths moving faster than any waiter. Princes and princesses with nervous tics.

A bartender paused in flight to take my order for a Tuborg. When he brought the beer, I asked for the boss.

"Mr. Tarra? Comes in about six, maybe. I'll tell him."

I had two more slow beers. At six-thirty a man stood at my elbow. Short and heavy, in a brown suit, he looked out of place among the flush patrons.

"You want Mr. Tarra?"

"I'm looking for Judy Carlos. Paul Shaw, a private investigator."

"Can I see your stat?"

I showed him my license. He nodded, and led me through the quieter club section into a curtained corridor. Halfway down the corridor he stopped me for a moment. I knew that some electric-eye device had just checked me for weapons. The heavy man knocked on an unmarked door. The door gave a click, and my escort vanished. I went into a pleasant office with two steel-shuttered windows. The man behind the desk was working on columns of figures. He didn't look up.

"Sit down, Mr. Shaw."

I sat. He went on with his figures. I sensed that he wasn't trying to psych me, or impress me, he was really working. When he reached a point at which he could stop, he pushed the papers away.

"Now. I'm Emil Tarra. You want Judy Carlos?"

The undertone of an accent, both foreign and unedu-
cated, and he was bigger and younger than I had thought
at first. Iron-gray hair going white, and deep creases in a
Latin face, made him seem sixty, but his voice and movements were no more than fifty. His dull, loose-fitting blue
suit covered good shoulders without fat.

"I'm trying to find her," I said.

His pale eyes thought about it. I remembered old men
who dozed in the sun of a Sardinian village: poor and
harmless. They were poor, yes, but they weren't harmless.
Old bandits, and hidden behind their sleepy eyes were de-
grees of ruthlessness unknown in softer worlds. They could
kill in a flash, without rancor, and sleep like babies. They
had neither fear nor hate, only a code of what a "man" did
in their world. Tarra looked like those old men.

"Why?" he said.

"She's vanished. Her husband wants to find her."

"How long since she was seen?"

"Two weeks."

"The same as here," he said.

"It looks like she was last seen here."

"That so?"

"You never wondered why she didn't come to work?"

"They come, they go," he said.

"No," I said, "not Judy."

"The husband says she's different?"

"I say so," I said.

"So? Like that, Shaw?"

"Like that," I said.

"What do you expect from me? I told the husband all I
know—she left here one night two weeks ago. Who knows
where?"

"What did Judy do here?" I asked.

"Camera girl. We've got two. Judy could con the gold out
of a mark's teeth. She worked the shift to midnight."

"What happened the last night she was here?"

"Nothing."

"She left at midnight, as usual? Alone?"

"Far as I know."

"I've got a hint of something wrong between her and Frank Carlos. Did she have another man, Tarra?"

His thin, perpetual smile changed without changing. The shape of the smile still on his face, but the "smile" gone out of it. He leaned toward me, his hands bending a paper clip.

"I like Judy, Shaw. What she does is her business to me. No one else's, not even her husband's. Okay?"

"No," I said. "It's two weeks, and that's too long. I don't care about Frank Carlos, I don't know his motives. I'm working for Judy. She could be in danger, or in trouble."

"That's too bad," he said. His pale eyes never moved. His hands twisted at the paper clip.

I said, "Frank Carlos was stabbed early today. He's not dead yet, and that's the only reason the cops aren't already here looking for Judy, too. They won't waste time until they hear what Frank can tell them, or until he dies. I don't have time to wait. I'm not sure what Carlos will say."

"You think Judy did it? Maybe had it done?"

"If she did, I want to hear why from her. I want to hear her story first. There's always circumstances, but cops don't always care about them. Sometimes they shoot first, or twist the facts. If she had nothing to do with it, I mean to protect her. If she didn't do it, but is mixed in, she could be in danger. One way or the other, I want to get to her first."

"Yeh," Tarra said, "I wish I could help."

"Can't you, Tarra?"

"No," he said, and pressed the buzzer that released his door lock. "Let me know if you find her, okay?"

I went out. In the corridor, my heavy-set escort appeared. He convoyed me as far as the bar, a drink on the house. I took it, another beer. Judy had left work at midnight, as usual—and vanished. I was thinking about another beer, when the thin blonde stood beside me. She had a camera, and wore a pair of nervous eyes and little else.

"Smile," she said, and smiled herself. "Lou says you're looking for Judy? Let me take a picture, I'm doing her shift now. You a cop? Why do you want her?"

I grinned at her camera. "Private detective. Her husband hasn't seen her for two weeks. No trouble."

She snapped her picture, began to write on a card. "One of the kid waitresses, Gloria Kazko, quit that night, wanted a ride to San Perdido. For next mornin', you know? She asked around. When Judy got off at midnight, she told Gloria she'd drive her up to Perdido right then. So they went."

"Why did Judy want to go to San Perdido?"

She handed me the card. "Who knows? Take the card, pay me five. Judy said it was as good a time as any for her to go."

I gave her a five. "What kind of car was she driving?"

"A bug, VW."

"Gray?"

"No, red. Wait for your picture."

I waited. *As good a time as any.* Something Judy had thought about, and decided to do on the moment. Something she had not wanted Carlos to know, unless he had lied to me. If she had gone to San Perdido at all.

The blonde brought my picture. My smile looked like it belonged on a plaster dummy. I said, "What's your name?"

"Marge Donner. Judy was nice. That's all I know."

She went off with her camera, and I went out to the parking lot. It was dark now, the lot less crowded in the brief lull between cocktails and dinner. I thought about Judy and San Perdido and a young man in a yellow sports car.

I was out in the dark parking lot before I remembered that this lot had an attendant. He should have been all over me, eager for his tip. He was nowhere in sight.

But I wasn't alone.

9 🦅

THERE WERE TWO of them.

One was twenty feet behind me, crouched on the balls of his feet, cutting me off from the lights of the club. Something glittered in his right hand, held low.

The second appeared directly in front of me, big and broad, like a tall tree stump in the night. I had a glimpse of a thick neck, a hairless bullet head, and a black face. Offense is always better. I went at him, hooked a left, crossed my right, and hit nothing at all.

He hit my nose. I felt the blood spurt. He hit me on the left side of my head, a shade high.

I was down, feet in the air, my head banging a bumper. I was overmatched. I'm six-feet-three, one hundred and ninety pounds, and I don't knock down easily, but he was a better man. He was also too quick. He moved in before my feet had come down. I kicked him with both feet in his bull chest. He fell back, and I was up.

He shuffled in. I jabbed a left. He picked off my jab like a fly. My right hit air again. A fist like a boulder slammed into my ribs. Another crushed over my heart. I was down.

I had hit only air, and that was all. I was going to hit with him. I rolled under a car. He moved to meet me on the far side. I rolled back out the side I had come in under, and came to my feet running. The second man ran toward me with his knife glittering. He expected me to try to evade. I didn't.

I ran at him. Caught off balance, his feet going one way and his brain the other, I bowled right over him. I knocked him flat—but not before I felt a quick burning in my side.

Then I was on the street, running, holding my side where blood dripped down.

This was Los Angeles. A lot of cars moved past, faces gaping at me, but few people walked. The bullet-headed man didn't care about what people there were. He was behind me. But if he could outfight me, he couldn't outrun me. I ran the five blocks to my office, and left him out of sight.

When the lighted glass doors of our lobby were half a block away, I slowed to find my keys. The second man was there ahead. He had come some shorter route, and now ran in at an angle toward the glass doors. He had his knife. I ran again. The lobby doors would be locked at this hour. I had less than ten steps on him at full speed. The plate glass of the doors was much too thick. I had no time for keys. I pulled my head down, swerved, and went through the glass side panels next to the doors in a shower of shattered glass.

I fell, came up, and ran up the stairs without looking back. I fought the pain in my side. I reached our floor, hit our solid outer door—and bounced off. I hit it again. And again. It ripped open and I fell inside. I stumbled into Delaney's private office, got the gun out of his drawer, sat in his chair, held the gun in both hands, aimed it at the open doors—waited.

No one came.

Blood dripped down my face, down my side. Cuts I hadn't looked for yet began to hurt. My side. My shoulder.

No one came.

I called Dick Delaney at his home. I needed a hospital, but I wasn't walking out of that office alone.

10 🦅

THEY STITCHED ME, tested me, X-rayed me, and doped me up. No major damage. And I fought them. I had to get to San Perdido. I lost. Dick Delaney sat near my hospital bed.

"You'll keep a day," he said in the muted light of the room. "What do I tell Thayer when he asks who pays?"

"To hell with him," I said. I think I said it, the voice thick. "Carlos—he said anything yet?"

"A few hours ago," Delaney said. "My man in the Sheriff's Office gave me all they got. They only had minutes. Two men attacked him, he didn't see them. They wore stocking masks, some kind of robes, and used gloves."

My mind was in layers of cotton. "Then he knew them, yes. They didn't want to be recognized if it went wrong."

"That's how it looks," Delaney agreed. "The police know that the wife's missing, that's all. Carlos gave nothing more."

"Can we get to him yet?"

"No. He's not our client, is he? He's under wraps."

I lay back. I was on my own all the way.

"No idea who jumped you, Paul, or why?"

I shook my head. It was a mistake. I had to grit my teeth. "But they knew me, knew our office. They were after me. Not to kill, just to put me on ice for a time."

The drugs were fighting me under. "Dick, pick up my car, and then get me a different car. Not a company car. Check on the two who jumped me, see if they're known." And I described them.

After Delaney had gone, I lay flat. What I had really wanted was to be alone to groan in private. I wanted to sleep if I could. I slept. Dreamless, unaware that I was sleeping.

I moved my head, and Maureen was there. She sat where Delaney had. She looked good. Her red hair tumbled down her worried face. She wore a green winter dress. Her breasts stretched it nicely. She saw my eyes on her. She smiled and came to kiss me. She sat on the bed.

I said, "What time is it?"

"Three A.M., darling. Dick called me when he found you. Larry Geiger flew me out in his 727. How are you?"

Some friends Maureen had. Mr. Lawrence P. Geiger, president of Walsh & Geiger Steel, and his private 727 jet. Why not? She was Maureen Shaw, star of stage, screen, and TV. Toast of the theater world, and my wife. And what was Judy?

"Better," I said. The sleep had done it. I hurt, but the layers of cotton were gone. "Cuts, sore ribs, a torn shoulder, but no damage. The knife in my side is the worst. They're keeping me overnight for observation."

"Was it about Judy, Paul?"

"That's all I'm doing out here."

"Dick told me about the husband. Paul, what could be happening? Knives, beatings, guns? That's not Judy."

"No, it's not Judy," I said.

Dick Delaney came in then. He stopped when he saw Maureen, but she nodded him to her. He smiled at her, looked down at me.

"No make on your bully-boys," he said. "Not local. I've got a new, rented car downstairs, your bag's in it."

Maureen held my hand. "Can't you rest a few days, darling? We'll go down to Laguna. Isn't this a police case?"

"No," I said. "I was attacked to stop me looking for Judy. If she's on her own, then she's in trouble. She doesn't want to be found, she's hiding."

"From Frank Carlos?" Delaney said. "He wants you to find her, he was stabbed after he called you. It could be the same two men. Maybe she's afraid of Carlos. Wives can know things about a man he doesn't want known."

"Judy never hurt anyone," Maureen said.

I said, "Then someone else doesn't want her found, or doesn't want me to learn what happened to her."

"Oh, Paul, you don't . . ." Maureen cried, bit her lip.

Delaney said, "Who knew you were looking, Paul?"

"That doesn't prove anything," I said. "Anyone involved with her or Carlos could guess what I was doing. The registration in our company car would tell them who we are."

"Where does it leave you?" Delaney said.

"On my way to San Perdido tomorrow," I said. I didn't look at Maureen. "Max Alfreda says Judy was unhappy, not working well. He thinks it was over Frank Carlos, but who knows? A girl at her job says she went to San Perdido two weeks ago. Her boss, Emil Tarra, doesn't know anything, he says, but he knows something."

"You think Tarra's lying?" Delaney said.

"Frank Carlos was in prison for eight months. What do I know about Emil Tarra and Judy?"

We were all silent. Delaney didn't know Judy, but he knew our work. Look for the obvious, John Thayer always said, and when a woman is missing, and her husband is attacked after he hired a private detective to find her, the obvious is clear. Maureen and I knew Judy.

Maureen said, "Men and theater, that's all she really ever cared about. Love and her work, and they were mostly the same thing, Paul."

"But her work first, her art," I said. And was that it? Art before some man who wanted her? Maybe before Frank Carlos, so he—? I looked at Maureen. "I need sleep, baby, and so do you. Check into a hotel, not my motel, just in case I'm being watched."

"All right, Paul. I have some business I can do here. I'll wait for you, until you're ready to stop."

Dick Delaney took her arm. At the door of the silent hospital room, she turned. Her eyes were hidden. She told Delaney not to wait, she had a car of her own. He left.

She said, "Judy never could hold a man long, but she never really lost any of her men, did she? They went, but part of them always stayed with her."

"Not always," I said. "Or only a very small part."

"I wonder how small," she said, and she went out.

Alone, I lay back. I needed sleep if I was going to San Perdido in the morning. The dark TV set high on the wall seemed to watch me like a giant eye. How small was the part of me that was still with Judy?

11 ⨝

SAN PERDIDO SPRAWLED all across its dusty inland valley, yellow and brown and gray in the sun, surrounded by the fields and smoking industry it lived for. A grimy, monochromatic city of small business, and a cheap main street of bars, bowling alleys, and honky-tonks for the migratory hands and packing-plant workers. Neat, patrolled suburbs for the owners of the businesses and bars.

The campus of San Perdido State was on the edge of the ghetto—cheap real estate. The uniformed campus policeman at the gate was friendly, until I asked for Students for a Democratic Society. Then he looked me over and took down my license number. I was glad my gun was in my bag. He directed me, curtly, to a parking lot behind a steel-and-glass building.

As I walked, stiff and sore, around to the front of the building, students passed in small groups and pairs. They watched me with blank, withdrawn eyes. Inside the building, I located the S.D.S. room. Two girl students looked at me. They didn't ask what I wanted. They waited in silence for me to reveal myself. At thirty, I was a question mark.

"I'm looking for David Eigen," I said.

"We can tell you about the movement," one girl said.

"It's private business," I said.

The other girl said, "Dave lives at 323 Fremont."

"It's quicker to walk," the first girl said. "Past the Administration Building to gate six, two blocks off campus."

I thanked them, and went back out into the sun. As I walked among the students—lying on the grass, wandering, talking low, strumming guitars, studying in the sun—I was even more aware of the sense of silence. I had expected more noise, more signs of battle. The scars of last year were there—marks of fire, replaced windows and damaged walls, too many campus guards—but a calm hung over today. I felt like a man on a battlefield after the first wave of conflict has ended, aware that the troops are off in the forests re-examining tactics.

At the Administration Building, I saw the kites. They flew everywhere in the open quadrangle between the building and the gates. Hundreds of kites in the sunny sky like small children at play. But the flyers of the kites weren't children, and I suspected that there was the reason for the kites. The kite flyers mocked a world that told them to be children by playing this child's game where all the guards could see them, and where the administrators could look down from their windows.

Fremont Street was the city again. No trees, no grass, dirt in the gutters, the old houses turned into student rooming houses. Students played guitars on the steps, beat bongo drums, read in the sun, sat silent in the windows. It was a separate world from both campus and city.

Number 323 was peeling paint and had an overgrown and littered front yard. I found David Eigen's name beside the door. His room was on the second floor. There was no answer to my knock, but I heard people inside. The door was open. I walked into a large room.

There were beds, some ragged easy chairs, a hot-plate and refrigerator, tables and wooden chairs. Posters and giant photographs on the walls—Fidel Castro, Che Guevara, Huey P. Newton, others I didn't know. Shelves were full of books, pamphlets, mimeographed sheets. Two girls and two men sat at one table. They didn't look up as I came in.

One of them let a handful of thin sticks drop onto the table. They studied the pattern of the fallen sticks. They muttered, nodded, and the one who had let the sticks fall opened a large book. He read the book, and closed his eyes to think.

I said, "David Eigen?"

A girl said, "Not here."

I knew what they were doing. The book was the *I Ching,* the *Book of Changes,* and the sticks were the forty-nine yarrow sticks. For three thousand years Chinese in search of answers had dropped the sticks, and found references in the *I Ching* to guide them to what life should be and rarely is.

"You want Dave Eigen, man?" a voice said.

He stood partly behind me against a front wall next to a window that overlooked the street. A tall man, well over six feet and strongly built, his black face long and stern, with a large, sharp Arabic nose and distant eyes that seemed to see past me to some far point. Beardless, his hair thick but not Afro, he was about thirty, and his face had seen a lot of life. The face of a man who looked up at a giant mountain he knew he had to climb, lived only to climb, but who did not underestimate the mountain, or expect much for himself when he reached the top—if he did. A tragic face, haunted.

"I want to talk to him, yes," I said.

"Dave likes to talk," he said. His smile was so thin, it was barely different from a frown.

The *I Ching* readers dropped their sticks again. The tall Negro's eyes moved to watch them. Neither sneering nor approving. Observing the ways of children. Indulgent, but tired of such irrelevant action. He stretched his muscles as if he ached, and looked back at me. His clothes were nondescript—gray pants, a green shirt, no tie or hat, Wellington boots.

He said, "Cop?"

"No," I said.

He shook his head. "You're a cop. It's in the eyes, the way you walked in, sizing up people fast. I do it myself now. You learn something even from the pigs."

He had a quiet, almost soft voice. When he said the word "pigs," there were no overtones. A simple label, the way I would have said "doctors" or "Englishmen."

"A private detective," I said. "Does that make me a pig?"

"I don't know you," he said. "Some private snoopers know cops are pigs better than we do. I never figured if it's being a fascist makes a man be a cop, or if being a cop makes a man a fascist. The power to kick people, we figure's what it is."

The "we" tipped me—a Panther. "You know Pete Wallace?"

His eyes were steady, his face showing nothing, but now he focused on me. I knew more about his affairs than he had known. He didn't speak, he just waited for what I'd do next.

"We're old friends," I said. "Paul Shaw. I saw him in L.A. yesterday. He didn't mention me?"

"No, he didn't mention you."

"He was going to look around for Judy Carlos."

I got a reaction. He raised one finger to his nose. He rubbed his sharp nose, slowly.

"You came to talk to Dave Eigen about Frank Carlos," he said. A statement, not a question. "Frank alive?"

"How do you know he was hurt? I didn't tell Pete Wallace."

He had been a man talking idly to a stranger, only normally wary. Now he was something else: a leader talking in public. A man with a public position, alert to consequences, and no word was idle.

"You think the cops'd miss a chance to bust John Morgan and his brothers?" he said. "Frank Carlos was a better excuse than they need, Shaw. They were around ten minutes after they got the teletype from L.A."

"You're John Morgan?"

"Yeh," he said, his eyes not distant now, alert and interested in me. "And like I told the cops, I haven't seen Frank Carlos since he went to jail. Okay?"

Before I could ask about Judy, Morgan's eyes flickered past me. A pale youth had come into the room. He saw Morgan and me. No more than five-seven, with hollow cheeks and hooded Levantine eyes, and no muscles at all in his thin frame. His whole wiry body made up for its lack of muscle with energy. He seemed to be running even as he walked to us.

"Who's this, Johnny?" he asked Morgan. He was nervous.

Morgan told him. "He wants talk about Frank Carlos, Dave."

"Is Frank dead?" David Eigen said.

I said, "The police talked to you, too?"

"What else?" Eigen said. "What about Frank?"

"He's alive. I came to talk more about Judy Carlos."

"Judy?" Eigen said. "She's still not back?"

"You knew she was missing?"

"Carlos called us both," Eigen said. "Maybe a week ago. We hadn't seen her. You don't think she tried to kill—"

"Two men attacked Frank Carlos," I said.

John Morgan said, softly, "Men get hired, Shaw."

"You're saying you think Judy tried to get Carlos killed?" I said. "Why, Morgan? You have a theory?"

He didn't answer at once, his eyes back in the distance,

studying his own thoughts. "Judy been missing two weeks, yeh? Frank gets jumped. So you think it's the same people who jump Frank make Judy be missing. Only who cares about Judy, you know? Frank, yeh, we got plenty of enemies. But Judy? I don't see where Judy figures, Shaw, unless maybe she's mixed with someone is after Frank. Like, Frank's been inside for eight months, right? Maybe Judy met new people, changed her mind."

He was theorizing, but was he doing it for himself, or for me? An old theory, thought about before; or a new idea, spur of the moment?

"Why would she change her mind?" I said. "Change it about what, Morgan?"

"Maybe what she wants, maybe about Frank," Morgan said. "Ask Dave, he knows Judy better than me."

Dave Eigen jumped a foot. "You're crazy, Johnny! I mean, who knows Judy? I mean, for real, you know? All she cares about is her stupid theater!"

Eigen glared at John Morgan. The tall Negro didn't even notice, his mind busy, unaware of Eigen. Morgan was thinking. I had the feeling that John Morgan did a lot of thinking. I also had the feeling that David Eigen was afraid of Morgan. Uneasy allies.

I said, "You both think her being missing has some connection to the attack on Frank Carlos?"

"No!" Eigen said, too fast.

John Morgan said, "Maybe, maybe not, Shaw."

I said, "Frank Carlos knew the men who attacked him. That mean anything to either of you?"

Eigen shook his head, automatically. "No, not to me. How do I know who Frank knows?"

"How do you figure that?" Morgan asked. He understood what I was asking him—he knew Frank Carlos, and Frank knew him and his Panthers.

I told him about the masks the attackers had worn. Morgan closed up all the way.

"Frank's been away eight months," Morgan said. "He could know a lot of people."

It was a dismissal, and Morgan moved away from his wall. He did something, a reflex action, that chilled me. His eyes swept the street below the window—carefully. Automatic, with care to miss no enemy down there. I remembered Viet Nam. We had all done the same before we moved in those jungles.

Morgan said, "Tell Frank he's been on vacation long enough. When he's ready, we've got work for him here. You tell him."

He walked out without another look at me. I didn't try to stop him. It would have done no good. He wasn't a man who could be pushed.

12 ⌁

MORGAN'S EXIT LEFT a hole in the room. He had that kind of presence. The *I Ching* readers were still letting their sticks fall. David Eigen's dark eyes watched the door.

"You get nothing from Johnny Morgan he doesn't want you to have," Eigen said. "With him the fight's in the blood, in the bone. Cradle to grave."

"And you?" I said.

"All brain and history books," he said, a bitter tone of self-mockery in his voice. He had something on his mind. "I'm a rebel because I'm short, skinny, and ugly—didn't you know?"

I said, "Judy came to San Perdido late at night two weeks ago, Eigen. Monday night, February second. Why?"

"How do I know?" His voice was high, defensive.

"She didn't know many people here, did she?"

He was at the window. He looked down, but it wasn't enemies he looked for. He hadn't spent his life knowing that any man on the street could be an enemy. He was looking for help.

"No, not many," he said. The self-mockery in his voice again. "Busy, nothing but her damned theater. No art in you, she didn't even see you!"

"You keep saying that," I said. "Why did Morgan say you knew her better than he does? You're in love with her, Eigen?"

He turned. "Look at me. Look at Frank Carlos. She never sees me! She's nice, sure, doesn't even treat me like a kid. Treats me the same as Johnny Morgan, sure, but she doesn't know I'm around because I'm ugly and don't love her theater!"

"She wouldn't play, Eigen? Did you try?"

He shook his head. "All my life I've been told I'm an old man in a boy's body. I can hypnotize a crowd and negotiate with a sixty-year-old college president—but with a woman? Women look at me, smile, and I'm a kid! Damn women. With me she doesn't even talk, feel. I'm a hole in the air. In bed with Carlos, and who the hell else? Talks to Morgan, even to that old bastard Eyk. Not to me. I've seen her hold hands even with Eyk!"

"Who is Dr. Eyk, Dave?"

"Speech professor, a real smooth operator. Damn women!"

Was he really beating himself, or had he and Judy been more than he wanted anyone to know now? Age meant nothing, not to Judy: a lover of strays who did what she felt at all times, and instantly. Maybe Eigen had tried harder than he implied. Maybe too hard?

"You know she was in bed with someone besides Carlos?"

"No!"

"Why did she come here that night, Eigen?"

"I don't know. She didn't come to me."

"Meaning she went to someone else?"

"I didn't say that."

"John Morgan, maybe?"

"No!"

I said, "Pete Wallace said Judy talked about a man. A man she was seeing while Carlos was in jail. You, maybe?"

He was very pale. "Pete Wallace? You talked to Wallace?"

"Pete's an old friend of mine, Eigen," I said. "An old friend of Judy's, too. She talked about a man to him. Who?"

He turned back to the window, his shoulders shaking. He wasn't seeing the street below. He was a man who saw little but the landscape inside his mind. He spoke without looking back at me, getting control of his shakes.

"You see the campus out there, Shaw? The big question now is how to deal honestly with others. How to help. We want to have the world, but we want a world worth having. All of us, no matter how different our ways of getting it. We all hate politicans who want order before justice, so make a police state; an older generation that deep down wants tyranny. We hate education led by technicians and tradition-passers, not scholars. We're all outraged by an arms race when the world has enough arms now to destroy everything down to the bugs. We're sickened by a race war in Asia and a race war here."

He was on his own ground. The longer I let him go on, the farther down he would push whatever he had on his mind, what was scaring him. He was lecturing himself, building his strength, hiding his trees in a forest of ideas. I needed trees.

"Do you know a Gloria Kazko?" I asked.

He turned. "Gloria Kazko? No, should I?"

"Where were you early yesterday? Last evening?"

"Yesterday?" He seemed to think. "In the desert down

south, looking for fossils. I'm in anthropology. It's good to work alone on the past sometimes."

"How alone?"

"All alone. No one saw me Monday."

The desert was a few hours from Los Angeles. "You happen to drive a yellow sports car? Maybe have a friend who does?"

"A black MG. Plenty of yellow sports cars on campus."

"Nothing more to tell me? A hint? A thought?"

He let his hooded eyes wander toward the *I Ching* readers, who still sat with their sticks as if Eigen, John Morgan, and I had never been in the room. They still worked to find answers in a three-thousand-year-old book from a distant land.

"I didn't do anything to Judy, Shaw," he said.

I left him looking at the *I Ching* readers, but not seeing them. As I emerged into the street and turned toward the campus, the difference between John Morgan and me hit me like a slap in the face—I had not even glanced at the street for enemies. It was a white street, *my* street.

It was also David Eigen's street, and safe on your own street, it is simple to throw suspicion on an outsider.

13 🐾

THERE WERE FOUR KAZKOS in the telephone book for San Perdido, and none of them was a Gloria. I started calling. The first sounded like an old man. He had a shaky voice, and didn't know a Gloria Kazko but would like to meet her.

It would be nice to have a young relative. The second didn't answer.

"Yes," the third said, a woman, "I have a daughter named Gloria. Can I ask who's calling?"

"My name is Paul Shaw. I just want to talk to Gloria."

Silence. "Is she . . . Is it trouble . . . Her father . . ."

"No trouble, Mrs. Kazko. I'm looking for a woman who drove up here with her from Los Angeles two weeks ago."

Silence again. "Gloria doesn't live with us. Her father—"

"Where does she live, Mrs. Kazko?"

"Number 22 Glendessary Lane. I . . . ask her to call me."

"I will," I said.

The campus policeman at the gate gave me directions to Glendessary Lane. It was on the other side of the city, on the county road southwest toward the old mining town of Nugget that was a suburb of San Perdido now. A quiet, semi-rustic lane of small cottages and big mansions. The cottages had been for servants once, but both the rich and the retainers were gone, and the cottages were private homes.

Number 22 was a cottage set back from the lane among pines and some eastern oaks. It was pink, recently painted, but the garden had had only sporadic care. A red Volkswagen was parked in the narrow driveway. The car made me hurry to the door. It opened before I got to it. A medium-sized man in a cheap gray suit stood looking at me. His eyes were wide, all white and staring.

"She's dead," he said.

His hands moved like a deaf-mute using sign language.

"Who's dead?" I said.

But he didn't hear me. He heard nothing, really, except some kind of silent scream inside his brain.

"Dead," he said. "Gloria? I just came home. Here, not home. I mean"—his eyes puzzled—"she's dead . . . she was making lunch, and . . ."

I pushed past him. The girl lay on the kitchen floor. She had been making lunch. A carton of milk had spilled all across the floor, mixing with the blood. A full wine bottle lay near her, unbroken, as if she had tried to use it as a weapon. She had been stabbed. Not once. Over and over, and slashed, her back still bleeding.

The man was behind me. I whirled, but he held no weapon. He stared at the dead girl. A very ordinary-looking man, about thirty, but with the settled air that clerks and insurance men get. He sat down as if he had to think something out—carefully.

"She just got back two weeks ago," he said.

"She lived here with you?" I asked.

He said, "I mean, she wanted to go to L.A. and work, see some life, but she didn't like it, so she came back to me—you see? I live at home, my folks are old. I get a promotion soon, so we can get married."

"What's your name?"

"Fred Pacelli. I'm Catholic. So is Gloria."

"Do you know Judy Carlos? Was she here?"

The name seemed to break through to him. He nodded. "The girl drove her up. Two weeks ago. We moved in here. The old folks wouldn't like it, me and Gloria, you know?"

"Where did Judy Carlos go after coming here?"

"The girl drove her up? I don't know. Gloria went to her folks first, then I rented here. It was all okay."

He forgot me again. He sat and looked at the dead girl. The blood and milk didn't seem to bother him. I knew a man in shock, he wouldn't tell me much.

I found the telephone and called the police. Then I made a search. It was a small house, almost bare, as if they had just moved in, as Fred Pacelli had said. There were no signs of Judy, and nothing that told me anything except that Fred Pacelli and Gloria Kazko had lived here alone.

There had been no search, and no sign of robbery. There wasn't anything to steal.

14 ～

LIEUTENANT PATRICK DEVINE of the San Perdido detective division was tall, thin, freckled, and with thick red hair under his hat. He had a low, rasping voice. He listened to me when I told him I had come only to ask about a casual acquaintance of the dead girl's, and told me to wait. He was slow-spoken, neutral.

I waited in the living room while Devine set his men to work. They concentrated on the kitchen and fingerprints—they had seen that there had been no search or robbery. The coroner's man worked on the body, while Lieutenant Devine talked to Fred Pacelli. A quiet conversation, calming Pacelli. It took over an hour. I smoked a lot of cigarettes.

Devine pulled up a chair next to me. "He was like that when you found him here, Shaw?"

"Yes. What did he tell you?"

"Nothing," Devine said in his rasping voice. "Found her a few minutes before you came. Was at work up to twenty minutes before that. She's been dead a couple of hours."

"He have any ideas who or why?"

"No. Unless we find some prints or evidence, we'll have to do the routine on her life, look for intruders."

"No prints so far?"

"Looks like gloves. Now what about you? A case?"

I had decided about me. Carlos hired me to find Judy, and someone tried to kill him. Someone attacked me. Now the girl who might have last seen Judy was dead. Every hour Judy was sinking deeper. If I was to reach her first, I had to keep a free hand. I had to risk that Fred Pacelli was so far in shock, he wouldn't remember who I had asked about.

"An L.A. divorce case," I said, using my cover story. It was all I had. "A man whose wife thinks he was meeting a girl in a club where Gloria Kazko worked. The club told me Gloria had come up here. I came to see if she knew anything."

"Your man got a name?"

"George Hammond, 12 Mango Terrace, North Hollywood. Go easy if you check on him, okay? He doesn't know his wife has us watching him."

"I'll just have his movements matched to the time she was killed. You think he knew the Kazko girl could name his woman?"

"I don't know that she could, I never talked to her," I said. "The club has a lot of waitresses. I doubt if he knew Gloria Kazko's name."

"Probably not. What club did you say she worked at?"

Now I was on very thin ice. If Emil Tarra connected Judy or me to Gloria Kazko, my license was smoke. Then, Tarra hadn't seemed like a man who would say much to the police.

"The Carleton Club, in Hollywood."

"Okay, Shaw." Devine got up. He gave me a look. "I'll let you know if we find out anything. Staying in town?"

"No, back to L.A.," I said. How much was I fooling him? He looked slow, and sounded hard, but I began to think he wasn't either.

"You're lucky," he said, and glanced toward the kitchen where they were putting Gloria Kazko into a basket. "Some parts you never get used to. She was just a kid. Pacelli lives with his folks, works on someone else's money, and she was probably the first steady woman he ever had. Everyone got to have something good in his life. Now all he's got is columns of figures, a lousy paycheck, and a lease on this place."

He had forgotten me, and I eased out to my car. I wondered if John Morgan would have called Devine a pig? I didn't see Devine like that, but I was looking from a different place than John Morgan. A lot depended on where you stood.

Where I stood now, back in my car, was simple: in deep, and hanging by my license. Sooner or later the police would make all the connections to Judy. I didn't have much time.

15

Dr. Jonas Eyk, Professor of Speech, and the third name in the address book, was a trim, dapper man in his sixties. I found him in his office that overlooked the green campus. He wore a vest with his businessman's gray suit, a gold watch chain with a Phi Beta Kappa key, and rimless glasses.

"Yes," he said, "Judith was here about two weeks ago." He flipped his desk calendar. "A Tuesday, yes, the third of February. Early in the morning, I was late for class."

I let out a slow breath. He watched me from behind his desk without reaction. I smiled.

"I'd begun to think I'd never find anyone who'd seen her at all," I said. "What did she want, Professor? Did she say where she was going, or what she was doing here?"

But he had his own question. "Judith is missing, Mr. Shaw?"

"You didn't know? Frank Carlos didn't call you?"

"No. I've been away a week at a meeting. That morning was the last I saw Judy myself. Two weeks today, yes."

"What did she want, Dr. Eyk?"

"A social call, I'd say. Yet—" He paused as if to gather his words. A lecture-room mannerism. "As a matter of fact, Judy was rather incoherent. She rambled that morning. But, then, she usually did. Logic isn't her forte."

"Why did she come to you at all?"

"Why, we're good friends, you see? When she was on campus last year she often dropped in just to talk. An odd couple, eh? I'm all academic, a scholar. She is all non-academic, a doer. But I found her rather exciting, and it seems I reminded her of some man who had been important to her—in a fatherly way. At some eastern university. Rutgers, I believe."

Rutgers, yes . . . *"You should have known Professor Fraser, Paul. So strong, and so gentle. When my father left us, Mom worked for him, and I'd talk to him when I waited for her. He was the one who made me want to act, he loved theater. He showed me that the only real life is finding the power inside yourself. What the college boys did to me didn't matter. When I went down to New York at sixteen, Prof Fraser gave me five hundred dollars to get started. He made me look inside . . .*

I said, "How was she incoherent, Professor? Rambling?"

"I'm not sure. Depressed, yet voluble. I'd say she was trying to make some kind of decision, yes. I'd say it involved her husband, and possibly John Morgan and David Eigen."

"You're not sure? What kind of decision?"

He shook his head. "She was vague, perhaps purposely. Circling the issue, whatever it was. She did appear rather tired, not as well groomed as usual."

"As if she'd been up all night?"

"It could have been that."

"She never said where she was going? It's important."

"I can see it is," Eyk said, nodded, "but I'm afraid . . . I did gather an impression that she was intending to talk to John Morgan, or Eigen, or perhaps both. But I can't suggest she actually said that."

"No idea of what troubles she could have had with Carlos?"

"None at all."

"Did she oppose Carlos' part in the strike here?"

He laughed. It changed him. With his laugh, his face became a hundred percent less stiff, his manner freer.

"Far from it," he said, smiled at the memory. "She jumped in with both feet. Marched with the best and shouted louder. She helped set up a first-aid station, went from door to door in the ghetto. When it failed she was crushed, very bitter for a time, ready to start again at once."

"She believed with Carlos all the way? Was close to Eigen and John Morgan?"

"David Eigen wanted to be close to her, poor boy. She felt rather sad about him. John Morgan is close to no one outside his Black Panthers," Eyk said. "As for believing with Carlos, Judy isn't a woman who believes in programs or politics much, you see? Beyond her art, she believes in loyalties, the bonds of purpose, yes. Even bonds of violence, as we had . . ."

When was it, the day she marched in protest . . . *"They broke the march, Paul! They attacked us! Pete Wallace was hurt. But we stayed together. We were really together, devoted, helping each other. No one ran alone. It was wonderful. We all hide from each other so much today. There's so little chance to know each other. The violence made us trust, help, love . . ."*

Dr. Eyk said, "Judy is pure feeling, Mr. Shaw, all inside with her need to create truths. She wasn't so much with Carlos, as against the smug, comfortable, righteous people who hated the strikers, she—"

Her big eyes flashed at me. "I saw their faces, the 'good' people, hating us because we protested bad laws. Deep down they're envious, Paul, jealous! I've seen them. Inside they want to be violent, be free. They really hate the restraints they put on themselves, so they have to hit out at anyone who breaks out. They have to put their own chains on everyone! They hate anyone who breaks free!"

I heard her as if she were there in Eyk's office. For a moment I felt she was there. I blinked, looked around—

"Mr. Shaw?"

Eyk's voice came to me through a slow haze. He was watching me from behind his desk, the sun outside. He looked as if he had been talking to me all the time.

"Sorry," I said. "This is all getting to me. Judy and I, we were . . . close. Very close. A long time ago."

"I'm sorry," he said, and his voice had changed. A subtle difference, but I heard it. His voice stiff.

"You know Gloria Kazko, Dr. Eyk?" I said.

"Kazko? Not that I . . . wait, now. I believe Judy mentioned that name, yes. Some girl she'd been with."

"Were you alone when Judy came that morning?"

"No," he said. "My secretary was here. Some students."

Which would have made it unwise to hide the fact that Judy had been here. I said, "Does Judy have a lover here, Professor?"

"Not that I know. David Eigen, of course, wanted her." He hesitated, sighed. "Some months ago, while Carlos was in prison, she was here about some theater project. She spoke of a man who might be a chance for both herself and Carlos. The way she spoke, I sensed that this man was also a lover—you understand?"

"You know his name?"

"No, but she spoke of him more than once. I expect she felt somewhat guilty. I gathered that she had met the man where she worked, that he was well known at her work."

"In Los Angeles," I said. "You haven't seen her since?"

"No. As I said, I've been away, Mr. Shaw."

He didn't see me out. Five minutes later I was on the Freeway. I pulled off once to eat and rest. I hurt all over. I called Maureen at her hotel. She wasn't there. I left a message that I was going to miss dinner.

16 🪶

IT WAS DARK by the time I reached Los Angeles and The Carleton Club. The same running attendant took my car. He had a thick bandage taped on the side of his head.

"You got hit?" I asked.

"Last night. Never even saw the bastard. Some damned nut, you know? Didn't even take my money."

I sympathized, but I didn't tell him that I knew the men who had hit him had been after me, not his money. I walked into the bar and looked for my heavy-set escort of last night. He saw me first. I guessed that seeing people first was his job.

"You're Lou?" I said as he walked up.

"That's right, Mr. Shaw. You want Mr. Tarra again?"

"Yes."

He led me through the curtain into the back corridor, and we made our stop at the scanner that checked for weapons. Lou knocked on Tarra's unmarked door—a signal knock this time. The buzzer sounded. I went in alone. Emil Tarra was finishing his dinner this time, drinking coffee. He pushed a coffee cup at me. I nodded and sat. He poured my coffee. His pale eyes showed that this time he knew I was on more than a random fishing expedition.

"Find her?" he said.

"No, but I'm getting closer," I said.

"That's good," he said, sipped coffee. "The cops were around. They know Judy's missing. That's all they know."

"They'll know more soon."

"Is that supposed to worry me?" He put down his cup, leaned back. "You been acting like I should be afraid of cops ever since you come in the first time. What makes you figure I'm not just like any other citizen and businessman?"

"Any citizen doesn't have a scanner for weapons, a bodyguard, and a locked door that opens only from inside. My partner works out of Hollywood. He knows your record."

His eyes took on that sleepy look violent men get before they act. I've seen it on gunmen, fighters, and soldiers in the minutes before they move to the attack. He leaned forward and poured another cup of coffee. He drank, put the cup down, his hand still on it.

"You know, Shaw, I didn't figure I had to tell you the facts. Say I haven't spent my life making paper cups, and I maybe skate thin sometimes, what's that got to do with this?"

"You tell me, Tarra," I said.

He finished his new cup of coffee. "The law's a funny thing, you know? Take Prohibition. If I go out with a bottle, tell the judge I got a right to drink, I'd get slapped down. But if I sneak around selling booze, trying not to get caught, the cops don't worry too much. They chase me, but they understand me. Illegal, but normal—so long as I don't make it all too public, or break some bigger law."

He picked up the coffee pot. It was empty. He put it down. "The country and me, we think the same. A man makes his buck, feeds his family, sends his kids to college, takes care of himself. I say: Your law cramps me sometimes, so I'll beat it if I can, but it's your law, you got a right to make it. I don't stand up and say your law is bad, I spit on your law, you got no right to make that law. That's bad, dangerous. No one likes that, but the law and me know where we stand. Judy's private, Shaw, they won't push me extra for her."

"Unless she's part of your game," I said. "Or unless you're part of her private trouble. Were you her man while Carlos was in jail, Tarra? I know she had one. What did she do, say good-bye when Carlos came home? Was Carlos in your way? Or maybe you told her too much about your 'game' with the law?"

His manner slipped down to the bandit. "Out. Now!"

"No," I said. "Judy's not just missing now, it's not just trouble in the family. It's murder, Tarra. Gloria Kazko was killed up in San Perdido today. Where were you today?"

"Gloria? Killed because of Judy? You figure that?"

"Yes," I said.

He gave it his careful thought. No longer sleepy. He was adding the balance in his mind, the way he added his columns of figures. A businessman of odds and risks against profits and advantages. The balance came out in my favor.

"Not me, Shaw," he said. "That's a sucker game. I don't have to get my tail with married women. You want a blond, good-looking guy about thirty or so. Flashy dresser. Came here a few times. She went to his place sometimes. I had to call her there, had to go once: 1138½ Canejo Place, Santa Monica."

I didn't like the feeling in my stomach as I went out. A young man, handsome. Maybe a first love never really dies.

17 ❧

THE HOUSE on Canejo Place had only a small light on the first floor, but the second floor blazed with light—and noise. The ragged violence of a crowded party, and the volume of the Red Army Chorus. I was at the porch before I saw that it wasn't the house I wanted. It was 1138.

A cottage in the rear was 1138½. I circled the cottage in the night. There was no light or movement inside. I used my set of keys on the front door. I didn't worry about noise, the volume from the house would have drowned a dynamite blast.

I stood inside an empty room. Was it all going to be dead ends? The cottage was bare, not even furniture. I locked it as I went out and back to the front door of the house. A plump, middle-aged woman answered my ring.

"I'm looking for the people in the cottage back there."

"The cottage?" she said. "Do you want to rent it? It's vacant, we're redoing it."

"I just want the people who did live there. Have they been gone long?"

"A few weeks," the plump woman said. "Just him. Mr. O'Connor was a bachelor."

"Blond, good-looking, thirty-odd, an expensive dresser?"

"That was Mr. O'Connor. Very dashing." There was a wistfulness in her voice. Not that O'Connor would have dashed at her, but that she wished she still cared.

"Do you know where he went?"

"No, but George might. My husband, he's upstairs at the meeting. You could join the meeting, too. We're Buddhists."

I wasn't sure I'd heard right. Maybe she couldn't pronounce Baptist. Her plump pink face and motherly figure were right out of the Bible Belt.

"Buddhists?" I said.

"For two years," she said proudly. "*Nichiren Shoshu*, it means Nichiren's True Sect. He was a Japanese monk a long time ago. Thirteenth century, I think George told me."

She said *Nichiren Shoshu* as if it were some kind of cake she was baking for a church social down by the Wabash. I felt a little dazed. The feeling didn't go away when I climbed the stairs, and came out into a large room packed with some fifty people all on their knees in front of a table with two tall candles and a framed inscribed paper scroll on it.

"I'll find George," the plump lady said.

There were flowers all around, and the noise had changed from what had sounded like the Red Army all singing together, in what I realized now was a chant of some kind, to a wild community sing. I knew the tune they sang, but not the words. It ended, and they all shouted a cheer:

"Ay-Ay-Oh! . . . Ay-Ay-Oh! . . . Ay-Ay-Oh! . . ."

Lusty and enthused. Happy and breathless. As mixed a group as I'd ever seen: men, women, young, old, suits, sandals, white, yellow, a few black. I felt good watching them —they all enjoyed it so much; eager yet relaxed. They had strings of tassels and beads wrapped around their fingers, the tassels hanging down when they held their hands in a prayer attitude.

"Ay-Ay-Oh! . . . Ay-Ay-Oh! . . ."

Up front, the leader began a new song. The finale from *Hair*—"Let the Sun Shine In!" But the words were different—Let the Shoshu In! They sang with the abandon of drunken longshoremen, and a lot more enjoyment. The balding man who walked to me carried his tasseled beads and sang as he came.

He smiled at me. "Want to join up? Come any time."

"Not my thing," I said. Why wasn't it?

He said, "Not mine, hell no. Only two years ago I had blood pressure, a pain in the gut, and bad temper running two houses and a shoe store. Now I come to a meeting, feel good, calm down, and no more pressure, gut pain, or lousy temper. No color line, generation gap, or East and West. Just people. We even got a studio v-p. Small here, but growing. We're Buddhists."

"It's a long way from Zen," I said.

"What do I know about Buddhism? It works, this chanting, singing. Face it, churches lost my generation and all the new kids. Church you listen to what ain't worked in two thousand years. Here you get into the act, chant up a storm, everyone grins—and maybe it'll work."

"I'll try it sometime," I said.

"No time like now."

"Now I'm working." I showed him my license.

"Like that? Why you want Rick O'Connor?"

I decided on the truth, part of it. "I'm looking for a woman, young. Her father wants to talk to her."

"Judy?"

"You know her?"

"A couple of times, after O'Connor was gone to work, we talked. Nice woman. Too nice for him. What do you want?"

"Where I find O'Connor."

"Yeh," he said. "I been thinking about that myself. He didn't leave any address, but when I cleaned out the cottage, I found a typewriter. Never used, from the look. I called Judy at her club—she'd told me about the club. She said O'Connor'd be in touch. Next day a cab comes for the typewriter. Just a cab, empty. I sort of wondered, you know, so I asked the cabbie where he was taking the machine. He said 970 Canyon Drive, Beverly Hills. Take it to the back door. Funny, you know?"

"Yes," I said. "Funny."

He said, "Beverly Hills is some jump from here, from my cottage. It makes you think."

"Doesn't it?" I said. "When did you see Judy last?"

"Let's see, O'Connor moved out about a month ago, and Judy wasn't around a couple of weeks before that. When I talked to her on the phone, she said she didn't think we'd see her again."

"Thanks, Mr.—?"

"Carey," he said. "Carey the Buddhist. How's that?"

"Why not, Mr. Carey?" I said.

I went out as the current song ended, and down the stairs to a chorus of:

"Ay-Ay-Oh! . . . Ay-Ay-Oh! . . . Ay-Ay-Oh! . . ."

In my car, I got my Colt out of my bag and strapped on my shoulder holster. I loaded the pistol. It was a long jump from the cottage to Beverly Hills, but a short drive. As I drove I wondered if Judy had made the jump with O'Connor. If there had been a jump. Maybe O'Connor was the gardener.

I didn't believe that, Judy wasn't a woman who met gardeners much. I also didn't believe Judy was a woman who would buy Beverly Hills.

I had been wrong before.

18 🐚

WHEN I SAW THE HOUSE, I knew O'Connor was no gardener. It was a rich house—palms, lawn, flowers, pool, the works—but not big enough, or rich enough, to have a permanent gardener. It, too, blazed with light and noise, the blue pool brilliant with underwater lights and floodlights.

As I walked from the street I didn't think this noise was a Buddhist meeting. A more familiar noise—the whirl of a Beverly Hills party. Cars were parked all along the driveway and in the turnaround. I rang at the front door, thinking about what I was going to say to O'Connor when I found him in the middle of a party. I had to ring three times, and had plenty of time to think.

When the door opened, I didn't have to think any more.

. . . Judy said, *"Would you have wanted me a virgin, Paul?"* I said, *"I don't know, honey. Maybe."*

"No, darling," she said, touching me in the dawn light of her room. *"A girl who never makes love to anyone but the first man stays a girl,*

closed up, narrow about life. It's the moment of that second man when she becomes a woman, grows up, can give as much as she takes."

"Am I the second, Judy?" I said. "After Rick Elliot?"

"No, and that doesn't matter," she said. "I hate Rick. He's so empty, so hollow. Only I wanted him, too. I need him to want me, Paul. I need to be chased, taken, eyes on my body. Ever since those college boys at Rutgers who used me when I was the town easy mark, and laughed at me with their plaster virgin dates. I need men to want me, and I hate it, too. I won't use sex to get ahead, but I need men, and sometimes I cry when I do. I cry, but I go back to them."

"No more, Judy," I said. "No more after me."

"We're special, Paul, but I know myself," she said, and kissed me. "When it happens, will you understand, Paul?"

He stood with a glass in his hand in the open doorway of the rich, noisy house. Blond, handsome, flashy—and his name wasn't O'Connor. The man I took Judy from—Rick Elliot.

"Hello, Elliot," I said.

He didn't recognize me, Rick Elliot. Who was I to him? A brief incident among many a long time ago.

"Sorry"—his masculine voice thick—"do I know you?"

"Paul Shaw," I said. "Where's—"

He swayed a few inches. "Shaw? Any relation to the great Maureen Sh—"

We all have keys to our memory. For him, now, it was Maureen. Her name sent his mind back nine and ten years, and killed all the whiskey. Once, at a business party, I met a man I'd known when he was a young junkie living on handouts in doorways. He was with his new wife, and the party was given by his boss. The terror in his eyes when he realized when I'd known him was the same terror I saw in Rick Elliot's eyes.

"What . . ." he stammered, "what do you . . . ?"

"I want Judy," I said. "Judy Carlos, Judy Tower—what name did she give you this time? I want her fast."

"Carlos," he said, and wiped his face. "Come in. Left, the office, my wife is . . . Please, Shaw."

I went where he pushed. In the big living room, someone was playing the piano, two couples were dancing without shoes, a young girl sat on the piano singing to herself, couples and loners drifted in and out of the house through French doors, and in the main pack they stood hip to hip with raised glasses and moving mouths. They all glittered with jewels and beautifully capped teeth, the clothes on their diet-slim backs, male as well as female, could have fed most of Watts for a week, and none of them even looked at me.

Elliot closed the door of his neat Bauhaus-modern office. The noise faded to a low rumble outside. He leaned with his back against the door, as if to defend the gates. I sat on his desk and watched the whiskey sweat out of his face.

"Where is she, Elliot?" I said.

"How do I know? Her husband got sprung."

"You just walked away? Convince me."

He crossed to a chrome-and-brown couch. He walked as if an audience were watching. He sat, and took a drink from his glass as if closing a deal. "I've got a wife and kids. Okay, I like the free stuff too. I direct now, produce on TV, my own production setup. Big, and pots of loot. I can help an actor. I can get you work, plenty. Your wife, too, big as she is. I can get her contracts she'll drool for. You name it."

"I don't act any more, Elliot, and my wife doesn't need your pennies," I said, and said, "I'm a private detective now."

He jerked on that couch as if I'd slapped his face, hard. I could almost hear the sound of the slap. His eyes ran for cover. He drank, convulsive, the deal turned down. His face went through so many changes he could have been auditioning a scene for me. It settled on anger.

"The damned bitch! What does she want? Money? Contracts?" He had a one-track mind that had bought and sold too much flesh, had been bought too many times itself. "A writing contract for that husband? His plays stink, she knows that herself, but okay."

"Judy said Carlos' plays stink? I don't believe that."

"So don't believe! She said it."

"How'd you run into her?"

"In The Carleton Club. My wife was on one of her 'vacations' at Palm Springs. Judy came up to take my picture— bingo! I wish to God I'd never seen her tail again." Self-pity, he had it all. "A guy doesn't forget Judy. One look, I could feel her down where it counts."

"She was glad to see you?"

"Judy always liked me in the sack." He smiled with the pride of a field hand. The smile faded even as I watched. "Damn her! Always did make me feel I was only a hunk of meat. You know what she said when I asked? 'We might as well, I know I will anyway.' Like I tasted bad, but she'd do it anyway."

"At that cottage?"

"Maybe ten times, no more. Now she wants to squeeze me. Go on, tell me what the hell she wants from me."

"I'm not working for Judy, Elliot, I'm looking for her. She's missing, vanished."

The fear came back in his eyes. "Missing?"

"I asked where she was. You don't listen too well."

I doubted if Rick Elliot had listened to anything but his own voice, inside or outside, all his life. The fine sounds of his own schemes and ideas drowning out all else. Now he had to hear, and what he heard scared him.

"Missing?" he repeated.

"Two weeks. When did you see her last, Elliot?"

"Months ago! I swear. Six, seven weeks at least. I even got rid of that cottage. Finished, you know?"

"You rented the cottage just for Judy to visit?"

"Sure, it makes it easier. Damn near wasn't worth it."

"What do you tell your wife?"

"Joanne? She's too busy having fun on my money to ask questions. I have to work on rewrites, adaptations. I get paid extra for doing scripts; Joanne likes that. I tell her I have to hole up to write. I take a typewriter."

"But Frank Carlos came home, and she broke it off?"

"Pfft! Like that, no matter how much I called her."

"You called her at her home?"

"Hell, no. At The Carleton Club."

"So she just cut you off? That's twice she did it."

"Three times. After you left her back then, we had a rerun for a year or so."

His deep voice carried echoes of the past and his whiskey eyes seemed to be seeing better times. He was a man who had it all, but nothing would ever be exactly what he wanted. No one had ever revealed to him what he really wanted.

"Three times?" I said. "So she broke it off again? That can affect a man. Too much, the last straw."

"Jealous? Over tail? Hell, there's always more."

"But some men get hooked on a special brand, like a drug. Where were you on the third? A Tuesday."

"Of February? Christ, how do I know?" He crossed to the desk where I sat, pawed through a leather appointment book. He looked at a page.

"Well?" I said.

He licked his lips. I pushed him aside. The page for February 3 was blank except for a single letter, *J*, and a dash. The page for February 2 had a note on it: *Joanne to Palm Springs, call her.* The pages for the fourth and fifth were blank.

I said, "You write out your wife's name, not just 'J.' "

"Listen, Shaw, I—"

"You listen! Frank Carlos is almost dead, and a girl who just barely knew Judy is dead! I'm not playing!"

He sat in his desk chair. "I'd forgotten, I swear. It didn't come off. I called Judy, set up a date. I talked Joanne into another Palm Springs trip by herself. I never could get Judy out of my mind. Maybe because she never *saw* me, looked right past me even in bed! I was going to talk her into going down to Tijuana, away from Carlos. Tuesday night."

"She agreed to meet you? Go with you?"

"Not go with me, I hadn't suggested Tijuana, not yet," he said, and clenched his teeth as if he wished he didn't have a tongue. "Look, all right, she wanted me to get work for Carlos, buy his scripts. That's why she agreed to meet me, I know that. I . . . was going to use that to talk her into going to Tijuana."

His handsome blond head hung down. He wasn't ashamed of pressuring a woman into bed, he was just ashamed to be made to talk about it.

"She didn't come?"

"No. She called at eight o'clock, from San Perdido. She wasn't even in town! She sure had me on her mind."

"You were pretty angry?"

"What do you think?"

"So mad you went to San Perdido to find her?"

"So mad I got drunk. Right here."

"Alone?"

"Yes, alone. I was alone all next day, too. I'd arranged to be free to have time in Tijuana, right?"

It didn't help him, or me. No alibi. Well, few people had alibis when you came down to it. Not innocent people. The guilty usually did have.

"What did she say on the telephone?"

"The date was off, what else? She'd have called me earlier, but she got tied up with her crazy Panther buddies!"

I was off the desk. "She said she'd been with the Black Panthers? With John Morgan, maybe?"

"I don't know, yeh, I think she said something about Morgan, and that S.D.S. bum Eigen, too. She was with the Panthers when she called, couldn't talk much. Said she'd see me Wednesday, but she never showed then, either."

"You know John Morgan and Dave Eigen?"

"Hell no, but she talked about them. I know their kind. Big winds can't make a dollar, so have to tear down. She talked my ear off about them and that strike. She always was one hell of a talker in bed, you know?"

"I know," I said. Sex, art, and life were all one to Judy. "She'd wanted you to give Carlos work from the start?"

"No, she started on it a month before he got out. It seemed important, that's why I figured to use it to get her to Tijuana."

"What did she say about Carlos and his work?"

"Not what she said, the way she acted. Like she was in a box and had to bust out. Like to bust free, she had to get Carlos theater work."

"What did you say?"

He shrugged. "Told her I'd try, but if she got rid of Carlos, I could get her work for sure."

"You're a sweetheart," I said.

He hunched in the desk chair as if cold. "A cheap louse, she said that. Nothing hidden about me, she said. I was just what I was, I—" He looked up at me again, a sudden puzzled look. "She said I had nothing hidden—not like some others."

"Others?" I said. "What others? Hiding what?"

"Wait." He closed his eyes, seeing it. "She said . . . there were lice in every good fight, a . . . a slimy underbelly of every right cause . . . Yeh! Fakes. A . . . a pig behind too many nice, smooth fronts. Liars. Yeh . . . just like that, she said it." He opened his eyes, looked up. "It was right when she asked me to help Carlos. I said I'd rather ditch Carlos and help her. I said she knew his scripts were lousy. She said he'd get better, he would be good, and she knew good from bad. Then she read me some crap script she had in her bag —half-crazy junk. Not Carlos' stuff, some other junk. She got mad when she read it; you know Judy and her art."

"Whose script, Elliot?"

"I don't know. No one special. Someone she ran into. Maybe at her club. Or maybe it was that nut Max Alfreda. She was going to see him Wednesday before she came here."

"And she never came here on Wednesday?"

"No. She was due at noon, I gave her until twelve-thirty. Then I went driving. She never even called that time."

"You went driving? Where did—?"

His whiskey eyes dilated, then went into hiding. He smiled happily at something behind me. I heard the door close.

She was tall and blond. A big woman, all curves and without fat. Her face was beautiful. It had a lot of care. Elliot was making more money than I'd thought. Some men never seem to know how good they have it, always want what's outside their garden. Then, who could really know what another man's marriage was like?

Elliot was up, all smiles. "Come in, sweetie."

She came in, calm and stately. "I just wondered where you were, Richard. You have people to talk to. Evans wants you."

She spoke like a matriarch instructing a dull son-in-law. I guessed that whoever Evans was, he was important. She had a good thing, and she intended to make sure it stayed good—or got better.

"Coming now, sweetie," Elliot said. "This is Paul Shaw, an old friend from New York. My wife, Joanne."

I said, "Mrs. Elliot."

Her china-blue eyes estimated me. I recognized her as one of those women to whom the words *man* and *husband* are identical, and a new man is instantly rated for that status. Sex doesn't enter the picture. I felt I passed the genes, public-escort, and grooming standards, but failed Dun & Bradstreet. She turned her bone eyes back to Elliot.

"The good old days, dear? Those friends were mostly women, I thought? All the ingénues."

"I was a rest period," I said.

She stiffened. She didn't like sarcasm. She said, "Shaw? Do you know Maureen Shaw, perhaps?"

"My wife," I said, resisting temptation to wit.

"Ah?" I went up a few notches by association. "We've never met her. I know Richard would love to meet her, wouldn't you, dear? Richard would love to work with her."

She put a reading on the word "work" that told me she at least had ideas about her husband's ways with women. It didn't sound as if she cared much. That cottage might have been a waste of good money.

"She doesn't care for TV," I said. "She likes to act."

Her eyes said that she didn't like me much. Downgrading her husband's profession and status downgraded her. If the attitude spread, it could downgrade her income and privileges. I wouldn't have wanted to be in her way if she felt I was a threat to her privileges. Now I was only a threat to her plans for the rest of the night.

She touched Elliot. "We must get back, Richard."

"I was just leaving," I said. "I'll be around, Elliot, in case you want to discuss anything some more."

My departure caused no more stir than my arrival had. They were heading for the pool now, stripping or not, depending on their whim. Like eagles at play, they knew their invulnerability. But I had caused a stir in Rick Elliot. One way or the other, he wouldn't sleep well for a few weeks, and on my way down the car-crammed drive I wondered if Judy had showed that Wednesday after all.

Elliot was weak, but he would be dangerous if badly injured in a vulnerable spot. We all had our dangerous points—what was Elliot's?

Joanne Elliot might not care what her husband did with his male attributes, but she cared a lot about the possession of the rest of him. She had been in Palm Springs. That wasn't far.

My shoulder and head had begun to throb by now and

my side felt wet. The wound had opened some, I had been on my feet too long for one day. But in my car I looked across the dark and quiet street to the bright, noisy house. A nice house and a nice life. A man, or a woman, could do a lot to hold onto that house and life, if Judy had showed that Wednesday.

19

ONLY THE OLD PORSCHE was in the dark parking lot beside the The Theater of Elemental Force. The shabby mansion itself was dark, but I heard voices. Rising and falling voices in a strange debate that was half-chant. Not the happy chant of the *Nichiren Shoshu*. A black chant, lunatic, undulating like a snake in the night.

I went up the porch steps and into the dark foyer, and I realized that the voices were all one voice. High and low, bass and falsetto, coiling around itself. The agony of two hands on the same body clawing at each other.

It came from the theater side of the black foyer. The double doors were closed. I pushed them open as quietly as I could. The theater was all in darkness except in the center where the raised levels of platforms stood. There, a single baby spot made a shaft and pool of light that illuminated Max Alfreda. He was half crouched, twisted, peering out toward a dark corner of the rows of seats, still in his brown monk's robe, like a scene from some savage performance of *Macbeth*.

His two voices seemed to play with the echoes of the

darkened room. I stood just outside the opened doors. He held his twisted crouch.

His arm shot out toward the shadows, one bony finger pointed, his wrist arched like the esthetic wrist of a ballet dancer. The bass voice boomed, "Destruction is in you! The core of what we call life, the core of what must be theater. A disease, the theater, as vile as life itself."

The falsetto, piercing, "Viler! Oh, make my work far more vile than life, or how am I to cure, to reveal the beauty beneath the disease we now call life, eh?"

A high laugh that cut through the throb in my head like a hot needle through my eyes. He limped in a circle, in and out of the shaft of light on the platforms, and came motionless, standing tall and arrogant, his head cocked to his high shoulder.

"Life is disorder, yes," the falsetto brightly thin. "Then theater, mark you, is to be the more violent disorder that will release the energies in us, the hidden horror! Ah!"

He whirled in a pirouette, a descending spiral that ended with him on his knees, both arms extended toward the same dark corner of the small theater. He had amazing physical strength. His bass boomed out toward the dark:

"In the grip of a sacred disorder, yes. Insane, I know. You know. Rape, cruelty, mad violence, that is our fate. That must be our theater. To learn. Plunge into your evil, emerge to strip us clean. Insane evil, there is no cure but to see, feel, know it in us all."

As his bass voice echoed, he slowly lowered his arms until his hands touched flat to the wood of the platform. Head down, he kneeled there, silent. I stepped through the door, walked down the aisle between the rows of chairs.

He had not heard me; his falsetto cried to the shadows: "Monster . . . yes . . ."

He heard me. His deep eyes as flat as two black stones in his Indian face.

"Is this part of your work?" I said.

Bent like a hawk about to pounce. "I must work, yes."

His face glistened with sweat in the shadow of the high hood. His body trembled, but he breathed lightly after exertions that would have had me panting, if I could have done them at all. It wasn't in his body, it was in his will.

"It's not easy to take," I said.

He watched me. "It is not intended to be easy," and leaped up from his crouch, arms spread wide. "Violence, yes, it will not be easy, it will be only life and my theater! Ah!"

I said, "Did Judy come here on Wednesday the fourth?"

"Primitive," he cried, falsetto. "Incantatory! Elemental!" He dropped his arms. "I do not know dates. She is gone."

"The Wednesday two days after you say you saw her last," I said. "Did she come here, Alfreda?"

"I said she did not. She did not return."

"She was going to talk to you about some scripts."

"Scripts? I use no scripts, no text, all false." He dropped to his hands and knees, paced like an animal up and down the levels of the platforms, as if he could not break the mood of his work. "Realism is false, life is not realistic." Pacing on his hands and knees, up and down in the shaft of light. "The reason is a lie, there are no coherent characters. There is only darkness inside, and the magic."

"Were they Carlos' scripts?"

"A talent, Carlos, without direction or purpose." His lips skinned back, savage, and his body still trembled. "Attack, that is the way! Attack their blindness of logic, of harmony, of purpose, of reason that hides the truth. The horror."

He shivered, rose to a squat, his head moving back and forth from side to side as if he wanted to shake the head off his body. His coal eyes staring at nothing, and yet at everything, as if he knew too much horror, had seen too much horror through the sweat of his vision. More than he wanted to know or face, but had to face if he was to be honest in his art and his life.

"She didn't come that Wednesday? Call? Something?"

"She did not come." He remained squatting, bobbing his head, moving his shoulders, as if the mood of his work was a shield he did not want to lose, but his voice was losing that mood. "Violence and madness have been in the theater since the Greeks. It must be faced, used. Through the immersion in evil, we rise up purified. A theater must do no less than transfigure the audience that watches. The audience must go into the depths of its being, be transformed by what is beyond good and evil!"

His voice had risen, and the Nietzschean phrase echoed in the dark theater. He was explaining his work—and himself? Telling me something?

"The audience shares the crimes on the stage, sees the insanity in all of us that challenges morality. Camus wrote it in *Caligula*. Too rational, Camus, but an attempt to make the audience live the cruelty, understand the schizophrenia of that mad emperor, and release elemental forces that are in us all. To do this, I must understand the crimes of man, face the horror."

His hypnotic voice held me, and I heard the sound without recognizing it at first. A soft sound, light and quick, from a corner of the darkened theater. I jerked away from Alfreda's voice. Footsteps—hurried. Someone walked away out there in the shadows. I began to run. Alfreda's voice went on behind me as I pushed through the rows of chairs.

"Until we face the irrational, we cannot understand life!"

I fell over chairs, and pain stabbed the oozing wound in my side. I reached the corner where the footsteps had faded, and found a rear door. It was open. I ran through. A shape ran fast across the dark grounds of the theater. I chased, holding my side, my teeth grinding together.

Into the open street, and saw nothing. I stopped. No shape moved now in the night. To the right, across an open yard of another house, I heard the feet running. I went across the yard and over a fence behind the house into a second yard, and out into the next street. Cars passed, but no one ran. I walked half a block in each direction. I had lost him.

I went back through the yards and over the fence. My side was sticky. My mind raced as I walked slowly: had Max Alfreda known someone was in the theater? Judy? I had no way of knowing if it had been a man or a woman. What else did Max Alfreda know?

When I reached the old mansion, the Porsche was gone from the parking lot. I swore. At myself. Damn all!

In the mansion, there was no sound. Alfreda was gone. In the theater, I turned on the house lights, searched where the unseen listener must have been while I bathed in the flow of Alfreda's words. I found nothing, and went out to my car.

I sat in the car, lit a cigarette. I smoked, and let the pain ease in my side, the throb calm in my head and shoulder.

What now? After Max Alfreda? To San Perdido? If Alfreda had told the truth, Judy might never have left San Perdido. I knew that John Morgan and David Eigen were liars—unless Rick Elliot was the liar. The way you found who was the liar was to walk from place to place until the truth slowly separated from the lies. Police work.

I drove out of the small lot and found the first telephone booth. I dialed Maureen's hotel. She would be worried, and I needed to eat and rest. The hotel said she still wasn't in.

I called Dick Delaney's home. He could start looking for Max Alfreda, and maybe he had something to tell me about Frank Carlos. A child answered. Delaney was still at the office. I dialed the office.

"Dick? Anything on Carlos?"

His voice was tight. "Maureen's in the hospital, Paul."

"Maureen?" My throbbing head wouldn't focus.

"Paul, listen," Delaney said. "They found her in a restaurant parking lot. She'd been clubbed and stabbed. She's in surgery, but the doctor says she'll—"

"What hospital?" I shouted at the phone.

He told me. I don't remember if I hung up the receiver.

20 ～

It was the same hospital I'd been in. They told me to wait. I told them to go to hell. I got the doctor. One of them. Maureen was still in surgery. Dick Delaney flanked the doctor on the other side—more for the doctor's protection, I think, I probably looked pretty violent.

"She's serious, Mr. Shaw," the doctor said, "but not critical. She has a broken arm, head injuries, and a shoulder stab wound. Plus some minor cuts and bruises."

"Her face?" I asked. Not for me, for her. When you live with someone for eight years, you learn to think of what is important to them, to worry about that. Her face.

"No damage at all. She was very lucky."

"When do I see her?"

"After surgery she'll be in recovery at least an hour. You could go to our restaurant. We'll page you."

"I'll wait," I said.

"You'll eat," Delaney said. "You're not in such good shape yourself."

Delaney was right. There was nothing I could do now, and food would help. I was overtired and hurting. Just to sit down would help. We went to the restaurant. Delaney had eaten. While I ate the best steak they had, and as much else as I could, he told me what had happened to Maureen.

"She had dinner with an agent. When they were leaving the restaurant, the agent stopped to talk to someone—you know Hollywood. Maureen went out to his car. He followed in a few minutes, and found her on the ground next to the car. He must have scared off the attacker, but no one saw anything. The agent called the cops and an ambulance. Then he called our office and got me."

"No one saw anything?"

"Cops got ten reports of people seen running, all different. I gave the cops what I could without telling them what you were doing out here. I told them you were on the Hammond divorce case, the way we agreed. They'll talk to Hammond, but it's okay now, I've spotted his sweetie, we don't have to hide. He'll have a bad time, but maybe he deserves it."

I nodded, but my cover was getting thinner and thinner. My side was taking a beating, literally, with nothing much to show but dead ends and a single question—why?

"Why Maureen?" I said. "To pressure me?"

"Could be," Delaney said. "We can't keep Maureen out of the papers, Paul. I'm trying to keep you out, or most of California'll know who you are. The police are calling it a mugging for now. Maybe it was, Paul."

"You believe that?"

"No." He sighed. "Nothing stolen. A warning, I suppose."

"Maureen'll tell us when she comes to," I said.

Words are charms against fear and tragedy. I said "when," not "if"; pushing the fear far down into the depths of my mind; trying not to hear it whispering—if she doesn't die, if she doesn't die, if . . .

They paged me an hour after I'd finished dinner.

"She's awake," the doctor said. "Make it short. No questions, you understand?"

"How is it?"

"She should be all right," the doctor said.

"Should be?"

"We'll talk when you come out," the doctor said.

They had covered her head with bandages, the thick red hair I knew on the pillow beside me gone. Her left arm was strapped across her chest, her whole left shoulder and side heavily bandaged. The bottles and tubes that bring the fear up from your toes hung all around her. She opened her eyes. Vague, her eyes, as if seeing distances I could not see. She smiled.

"Hi, darling."

Her right hand raised toward me. I took it.

"How is it, baby?" I said.

"Fine," she said, smiled, unaware of how it was or even, really, that I had asked. "My poor baby."

"You look fine," I said. What else do you say? Inane.

Her eyes flickered. "I . . . they were there . . . they hit me . . . I . . ." A sudden, stabbing terror. "My . . . face . . . ?"

The hand I held squeezed; it was trembling. The left side of her hidden body moved, as if her left hand was trying to touch her face. I touched her face, smoothed the soft skin.

"All right, baby, it's all right. No damage. Not a mark."

Her mind couldn't focus long. She went limp. She smiled again, her eyes closed now. For a full minute she lay there as if asleep. I didn't move, held her limp hand. Her eyes still closed, her lips moved: "You must tell Judy about us, Paul. Soon." Lost from time.

"I will, baby," I said.

I held her hand until I knew she was really asleep. Then I went out to the doctor and Delaney. They didn't look happy.

"The wounds are all right," the doctor said. "She has a concussion and she's in shock. She lost blood. We won't be sure until perhaps tomorrow."

"Sure?" I said.

"I'm very optimistic, but nothing is absolutely . . ."

"You mean she could die?" My voice much too high.

"No, no. I'm sure, but with concussion—"

Something hit me on the shoulder. I seemed to fly. I was sitting on the floor against the wall, aware that I had fallen against the wall, slipped down. Delaney had me under the arms. I stood leaning on the wall. The doctor motioned to Delaney, and then I was in some kind of examining room. I had no shirt on. I sat on a table, my feet dangling. Something jabbed pain.

"A nice job you've done on those stitches."

"Beautiful," I said.

"I've restitched some. Now it's sleep for you."

I didn't argue. I found myself walking. Then there was air on my face, and lights rushed by. I was in a car, I decided with great logic.

I remember some stairs.

Then I was with them both—my girls. Maureen and Judy. It was the night Judy married, and the night she called to tell me . . .

21 ⌒

"I miss you, Paul," Judy said.

After she hung up I went to the windows. The black brick walls of the East Village were like ruins across the broken fences of the backyards. How many littered tenement yards had we looked at, Judy and I, in our two years? Maureen was there.

"Paul?" she said. "What is it?"

"Judy," I said. "She got married tonight. She called to tell me she misses me. Her wedding night."

Maureen said, "She'll be a good wife."

"That's all? She calls on her wedding night? She knows you're here, my wife? Still she calls me?"

Her face hazy in the dark, Maureen said, "To Judy, if it's true, it can't hurt anyone. Only lies hurt. She does miss you—on her wedding night more than ever, you see? She's in love, so she thinks of all love. Most of us have a past, we're formed by it. Not Judy. She has only a present—now. It's all now."

"She shouldn't have called me."

"Why not?"

"Because I have you," I said. "Us."

"We have 'us' because we have tomorrow. Judy doesn't ever have tomorrow any more than she has yesterday."

A light went on in a single window across the dark backyard behind our tenement apartment. Maureen's arms around me.

"Judy won't be chained," she said, "but she can't be alone. That's her complexity—her need to have someone, yet always be free. Maybe this time is different. This time she married."

"I hope so," I said. "I hope she can be happy."

"She's a girl we ache to see happy, don't we?" Maureen said. "I never knew anyone so made to be happy, just living."

I watched that single lighted window across our backyard. A lone light at 4:30 A.M. Who? Lovers now hating? Lovers loving? A poor couple with a sick child crying for help? A solitary man with intolerable dreams, unable to sleep? A man or woman, old or young, dragging up to go to work before dawn?

"When she was talking," I said, "I imagined her eyes, wide behind her glasses, staring at my face, wanting to know why nothing was ever right for her. Why didn't it ever turn out to be what she wanted? What was wrong with her that she could never be happy? Or what was wrong with everyone else."

Maureen said, "Come back to bed, Paul."

"Tomorrow," I said, "she'll bounce up eager for a new day. She always did. Then the new day will go wrong, and—"

"Come to bed, darling, now. We have us—now."

I went back to bed—with Maureen, loved her.

22 ∼

Awake, I lay without moving. *Why didn't it ever turn out to be what Judy wanted?* Bright sun in the windows told me I had been asleep a long time. It was Maureen, not Judy, in the hospital. I sat up. A motel room, my bag open on a stand. The motel Delaney had checked me into on Monday—a hundred years ago? The first time I'd been in the room. Some way to live.

I was out of bed when Delaney came in.

"She's sleeping," he said. "The Doc sounds cheerful."

"Where the hell are my pants?" I said.

"What are you going to do, cure her by a miracle? You need food. No hovering in hospital corridors counting minutes."

He was right. We had breakfast in some restaurant on the Strip.

"Find Max Alfreda, Dick. Turn the city upside down."

"Will do."

"Put a stake-out man on his theater. On Rick Elliot, too."

"You better fill me in. Who's Rick Elliot?"

I told him what had happened since I'd gone to San Perdido on Tuesday. His face smiled less and less. When I finished, I could see the wheels turning in his head.

He said, "Paul, does it give you any ideas? Carlos almost killed; you attacked; the Kazko girl killed; now Maureen. It's a lot of violence, action, for any one individual."

"You figure some organization? A group?"

"It's got the feel."

I said, "I've got to talk to Frank Carlos."

"I talked to his doctor. He's okay, but under guard."

"See what you can do, and find Max Alfreda, damn it."

He went, and I checked the hospital. She was resting. I sat around the office. I thought. The day passed.

Once I drove to the beach and walked. All the muscles and bikinis stared at a man who walked on the beach fully dressed.

At 2:00 P.M. I was back in the office. Delaney came in and slumped into a chair.

"No trace of Max Alfreda," he said. "I've checked every name I found at his theater. It's his home, too. No one admits to seeing him, Paul."

"You check a man named Keating?"

"No Keating anywhere in his papers, Paul."

"He's Alfreda's major angel. He should show in the records."

"I didn't find any backers in Alfreda's financial files. He seems to have his own money."

That jarred me out of my stupor. I got on the telephone to the major Cadillac dealer in Pasadena. I gave them a song-and-dance about working at a club where a Mr. Keating who drove a Cadillac had lost a valuable ring. I didn't know his name or address to send it back. They were friendly, Mr. Scott Keating was a good customer—a new car every two years, and always from them, the top dealers. I had figured that much. Mr. Scott Keating lived at 1430 Patrician Way.

The drive would do me good. I got onto the Hollywood Freeway, and then the Pasadena Freeway. A clear day, almost without haze, the way the city had been in its sleepy days before man forgot that nature hadn't intended the basin to contain so much industry or people with cars, had provided nowhere for the fumes to go. The Freeway ended in Arroyo Parkway. I made my left on Colorado Boulevard, my right into Linda Vista Avenue, and then blended into the green hills around the Annandale Country Club.

The house on Patrician Way was a vast red-brick pile trimmed in white, with columns and a long drive to the door. A four-car garage held the Cadillac and two other cars. A tall gardener stopped clipping bushes to watch me. I felt as if I should look for the service entrance, which always makes me march straight for the front door. A Japanese houseboy opened the door.

"Mr. Scott Keating, please," I said.

"Mr. Keating, he expects you, sir?"

"No, but he'll see me. Tell him Paul Shaw, about Alfreda."

The Japanese faded into the cool interior, and I looked over the entry hall. It was impressive, in the clean Federalist style of airy Eastern town houses. The houseboy came back and ushered me silently through the house out onto a brick terrace that overlooked a swimming pool blue and dazzling in the clear sun. Scott Keating sat in a deck chair, wearing trim gray slacks, a pale blue shirt so rich it seemed to catch a breeze when there wasn't one, and with a tall drink in his hand.

"Mr. Shaw, of course," he said. "Now I remember. Will you have a drink?"

"Beer, if you have it," I said.

He nodded to the houseboy. He was at home here, the master in his element. He wasn't alone, and I wondered how much a master he was. A woman lay in the sun a few feet away. She wasn't young, and her body in a bikini was too heavy, but it was tanned, oiled, and hard enough. She looked at me once, to check me out when I asked for beer. Her face was long and aristocratic, and she considered me carefully for a full minute. That's a long time to be studied. I winked. She didn't react. When she had seen all she wanted, she lay back and never looked at me or Keating again. He didn't introduce her. My beer came.

"Now," Keating said, "what brings you here?"

"Looking for Max Alfreda."

His pale eyes did a dance in his heavy pink face. There was something odd about him I hadn't seen in Alfreda's office—a juvenile air, boyish. The eyes of a boy looking out through his middle-aged face. As if he had grown older and richer, but the spoiled boy inside had not changed with the body. Not that he looked very old, no. A well-kept late forties. He drank from his tall glass.

"Why come here?" he said. "Alfreda never comes here. I wouldn't have him here, you know?"

"Too dirty, Keating?"

He tried a smile. "Too crazy. My friends would faint. We have rather different ideas of life here. More realistic."

"Profit and loss," I said, "with the emphasis on the former. Why do you give Alfreda money? It's not what I'd figure you to be involved in."

He stopped smiling, glanced toward the aloof woman, tried some bluster, but was still the boy inside. "Are you looking for hidden deviousness, Shaw?"

"Yes," I said. "I think Alfreda may be mixed in murder."

He lost all bluster. "Murder? You must be joking!"

"No, I'm not joking. A girl named Gloria Kazko is dead, a man named Frank Carlos was almost dead, a few people have been beaten, including me. On top of it a Judy Carlos is missing, and so is Alfreda now."

"Kazko? Carlos?" he stammered, drank. "What could I know about all that, for God's sake? You don't think—?"

"I think a lot," I said. "For instance, you said you were an angel for Alfreda, but his records don't show any angels. He spends his own money."

"His own money? No, no," Keating stammered. "We have a special arrangement with Alfreda, for tax reasons. I . . . we have a group, some businessmen. It's a tax setup for our private interests, you see? Each of us has his kind of hobby. Alfreda is mine. We pay him like an employee. That

way he appears on our books as a business expense. That's
why you didn't find my name in his records."

"That doesn't tell me why you back him."

"I . . . I always wanted to act myself. An indulgence. I
can't act myself, or work in theater, so I—"

"Buy your connection," I said. "Pete Wallace said that."

"Did he?" His eyes did their dance again.

"You don't like Wallace?" I said.

"I'm afraid he doesn't like me. I have nothing against
him."

"And you haven't seen Alfreda?"

"Not since that day I met you. I—"

The aristocratic woman moved her oiled body. She didn't
rise up or open her eyes. She just moved as if to get proper
attention, and spoke to the air: "We have an hour, Scott. Is
your business over?"

Keating turned and nodded as if she could see him. "Yes,
my dear. In a moment."

"Don't drag it out, Scott," she said.

He turned back to me. "I don't know anything about
Max Alfreda, Shaw. Just a small hobby. Now—"

The houseboy had appeared. I don't know how Keating
called him, or maybe the woman had a bell-button at the
pool where she lay. The houseboy stood like a Gestapo
guard. I guessed I was leaving.

"Let me know if Alfreda contacts you," I said.

"Of course, yes," Keating said. He stood up, gulped his
drink. He was anxious to get to whatever the woman
wanted him to get to.

I followed the houseboy out. The gardener watched me
get into my car and drive away. Keating was well pro-
tected. I drove out into Patrician Way, and turned left. I
saw the car.

An old black sedan that didn't look like it belonged in
this neighborhood. It was parked just up the curving block.
I saw what looked like four people in it. I watched the car

in my rear-view mirror as I drove slowly away. It didn't move to follow me. I wasn't sure, but what looked like rifle barrels seemed to be sticking up inside the car.

I drove slowly for a few miles, but the black sedan didn't appear behind me.

23 ~

THERE WERE NO CARS I could see watching our office. I went up and called Maureen. She was resting comfortably now.

At 5:00 P.M. the stake-out at Max Alfreda's theater called in. No one at all had appeared at the theater.

At 5:15 P.M. the stake-out at Rick Elliot's house reported. Elliot had nursed a hangover all day at the pool. Joanne Elliot had played tennis, and nothing else.

Dinner was at 7:00 P.M.

From 8:00 P.M. on I was at the hospital. Maureen was okay now, propped up, with pain in her green eyes now that the drugs had worn off. She wore lipstick. She was angry about her hair.

"It'll grow back, baby." I said. "You can wear a wig."

"Ten wigs. I can be blond, brunette, or even gray."

"How is it, baby?"

"Awful. Twenty minutes I get another pill, I hope." Her eyes closed. "There were two of them, Paul. A man and a woman. I didn't see them. They wore masks of some kind."

"A woman?" I said.

She nodded, her eyes still closed. "The man said, 'We don't want Shaw around, send him home.' They laughed at me."

"Do you want me to go home?"

"Yes," she said. "I want to take you home. I want you to finish this, too. Do your work, Paul. Find her."

"I will," I said.

She said, "Now go on. I'm going to start moaning soon, and I don't want you here when I do."

She held my neck in her one hand when I kissed her, pulled me down to her.

I went back to the motel. I went to bed. I slept badly. It was barely dawn when I gave up my uneasy dozing. I got up and called Delaney at home. He swore at me.

"Dick? You know Frank Carlos' room number?"

"Yeh, 224. He's under guard, Paul."

"I know. Call the hospital, get his nurse station. Tell them you're his doctor, you know the name. Tell them a Dr. Shaw from New York is coming to see Carlos in an hour."

"Okay, Paul. I hope it works."

So did I. Dressed, I drove out to the county hospital where they had Frank Carlos. Even at dawn the Freeway traffic was heavy, but my mind wasn't on the stampede we call living. It was on the woman who had attacked Maureen.

At the hospital, I slipped in without trouble. I tried four offices before I found what I wanted—a white doctor's coat and a stethoscope. I took off my holster and gun, and hid them in the closet of the office where I'd found the coat.

The deputy was outside Frank Carlos' room, dozing in a chair. I marched up to him.

"Dr. Shaw to see Carlos," I said.

"Identification, Doc?" He yawned.

I showed him my New York driver's license. He patted me half-heartedly for weapons. He had been told to expect a Dr. Shaw from New York. He nodded me inside.

24 ～

FRANK CARLOS LAY with his eyes closed. When I stood at the bed, he opened his eyes. His brown, pitted face showed nothing.

"I never told the cops about you," he said. "Where is she?"

"I don't know," I said. "You told the police that you don't have any idea where she could be?"

"I don't have."

"Someone tried to kill you, Carlos."

"Not about Judy."

"You don't know that."

He chewed at his mustache and said nothing.

"When I found you wounded in the Malibu house the first day," I said, "there was a young man down near your road. He was very interested in me when I turned into your road. He was sharp-faced, clean-shaven, broad but not too tall, long hair and Levis. Drove a yellow sports car. Know him?"

"He was watching the Malibu house?"

"I don't know exactly what he was doing, but he was there in the road, and he'd been up in the bushes near your house."

Carlos shook his head and winced. "Since the strike, all kinds come around me. I don't know that one. He could be anyone from the college, or just no one."

"Max Alfreda and Dr. Jonas Eyk both say there was some trouble between you and Judy after you got out."

He watched the wall again. I sensed that he was stalling. Why did he need time to think before he answered? A man can have a lot of reasons for chasing a missing wife, can hope for more than one result.

"They're wrong," he said.

"Are they? You know about Rick Elliot?"

"I don't know any Rick Elliot."

"Did Judy talk about getting you both movie and TV work?"

"She said something."

I told him about Rick Elliot. He didn't like it, but he didn't seem very surprised or especially angry.

"She vanished two weeks after you came home," I said.

"You think she went with this Elliot?"

"He says no, but he wouldn't say yes if it was yes. Why would she leave you so soon if it wasn't a man?"

"I don't know. Eight months I was in jail. She was alone. How do I know what she was doing? I didn't know about Elliot."

His voice carried more bitterness in it now, as if the fact of Rick Elliot had just gotten through to him. Or the fact of some other man more serious than Elliot.

"David Eigen was in love with her?" I asked.

He smiled. "Yeh. Poor Dave—a genius in one way, a kid in another. She pitied Dave. Nothing there."

"Maybe it was more than that on Eigen's side."

He didn't answer. Just chewed his mustache, said nothing. His manner and speech were disjointed, pieces that didn't blend.

"Did the militants use you in the strike, con you?"

"It depends on what you mean by 'con' me," he said.

"Does it have more than one meaning?"

He was a man who had almost been killed, whose wife was missing, yet his words were controlled, careful. Involved, yet impersonal, as if part of him stood aside and watched it all, including himself. Detached, or uncertain, or holding back. Perhaps trying to make some kind of decision.

"I supported the strike," he said. "I was angry. Then

Dave Eigen and John Morgan came to me and said that if I led the strike, we might win. I'm not an idiot, I know that you get nothing in this world without pressure. My name would get us the publicity, supply the pressure. Is a man 'conned' when he agrees to lead an action he already believes in?"

"I don't know," I said.

"Neither do I. The strike failed, I took the fall. Maybe whether I was conned or not depends on what happens next."

"What does happen next?" I said. "John Morgan told me to tell you they had work for you, the vacation should be over."

"Did he?"

"Why would Judy go to San Perdido on her own without telling you, Carlos?"

"She went to San Perdido? You're sure?"

I told him about her midnight trip and about her seeing Dr. Eyk. "Why would she go to Eigen and Morgan?"

He worried his mustache. "She never learned to cool it! Hell, I'm last year's news."

"Would the Panthers want to silence her? Some rival militants? Even the other side, the right-wingers?"

"I'm not that important."

"Maybe you're more important than you know, or more important than you're telling me." I told him about the attack on me, the murder of Gloria Kazko, what had happened to Maureen. "You recognize the two who jumped on me?"

His eyes seemed to both dilate and shrink. He moved in the bed like a bear trapped in a net. Pain made the scars and pits stand out on his face.

"No, I don't know them," he said. "You think they're the same ones who stabbed me?"

"I doubt it. My two acted like hired muscle, and they didn't use masks. I don't think they'd have been scared off just because you grabbed a gun." I told him about my last meeting with Max Alfreda. "My wife was attacked by a woman, as well as a man. Whoever was at Alfreda's didn't want me to see him—or her. Is Judy afraid of something, Carlos?"

He was silent; then, "Not the way you mean."

"All right," I said. "Now you're going to tell me what was wrong between the two of you."

He didn't thrash any more. "Give me a cigarette."

I gave him one, lighted it. He blew smoke. "Once Judy said to me that she could never hold a man. She could keep their desire, but not them. She sat with those big eyes behind her glasses, and wondered why men couldn't stay with her." He smoked, winced from the pain of breathing. "She lives in her private place, Shaw, her art. In the public world she's even naïve. She's not with our sweaty world. People have small needs she's blind to. They have schemes for things like power, success, fame, even justice. Most people work for tomorrow, the small comforts and status. Judy sees only today or eternity."

He was groping around for something in his mind. He would tell me when he knew just what he wanted to say.

"Yet she feels for the people, too," he said. "She wants to work for a better world now. She threw herself into that strike while it lasted, believed in it."

"And after it ended?" I said.

He didn't hear, or he didn't want to. He was telling the story his own way. "San Perdido is a hundred and fifty miles from L.A. She worked with me in the college theater, worked in a community theater in the ghetto. It wasn't enough. She felt we were at a dead end, out of our real work. Then she plunged into the strike. When it failed, she was more crushed than anyone. Judy doesn't think in terms of strategy, can't commit herself except to her art. When we lost, she felt it had all been a waste of time. When I got out of jail, her depression had come back a hundred times deeper."

"She wanted you both to go back to theater?"

He nodded. "She said we were artists, not soldiers. That was the timeless thing. She said artists had to sing, not rage. Find the whole truth for everyone. Sing universally, out of time, not fight against particular evils. She wanted me to drop out of any involvement with the militants, go back to the theater only."

He stubbed out his cigarette in a paper cup. "Dave Eigen and his S.D.S. people want me to go back around campus, be active, violate parole, try to get a circus trial like Chicago. The Panthers want me to join them, become a minister of information, and break parole. Then I'd go underground, or run abroad and make news. They all want my name in the fight."

"What do you want, Carlos?"

"I don't know," he said. "I want to write plays; I've been working on one since I got out. But I just did eight months in prison because I led a legitimate protest. We were right. Power beat us. After millions of words, and thousands of peaceful demonstrations, and growing violence, the Establishment still doesn't hear! I want human dignity for everyone!"

He lay back on his pillow. I let the silence hang. What would I have done? I didn't know.

I said, "Would she have gone to John Morgan and Eigen to try to make them stop pressuring you? Let you quit?"

"It's possible, I suppose."

"How hard would they try to keep you?"

"I don't know."

"If they're holding Judy, or scaring her into hiding, it would explain why they don't want me around. It might even explain why Gloria Kazko was killed—she knew too much. But why would they try to kill you?"

"They wouldn't," he said. "Or I don't know any reason."

"What if Judy's hiding out on her own, Carlos?"

"Then I don't know anything." He looked at me. "I was in jail for eight months. You say there was this Elliot. If she's on her own, then I don't know what's going on."

"I can think of one thing that might be going on."

"What would that be, Shaw?"

"Maybe you have a reason to find her you haven't told. That she knows things you don't want known, and she ran because she's scared of you. So scared she tried to kill you. I'm working for you. She could be fighting back, afraid of you."

He turned his head away. He was still weak and doped up, or he was just weary of me.

He said, "Then you better go and find out."

I went out past the dozing deputy. He barely noticed me. I got rid of the white coat and stethoscope and picked up my gun. Then I went out to my car.

The day was growing warm in the sun. I felt as if I'd come out of a tomb. I didn't shake the feeling the whole long drive to San Perdido.

25 ～

NUMBER 740 WAS THE LAST HOUSE on Fremont Street. Not that far from David Eigen's rooming house, it was a different world. Where Pete Wallace lived was the ghetto, and the house hung on the lip of a debris-filled, abandoned quarry. A small and shabby house, the yard a littered expanse of hard-baked dirt. The porch sagged and the house needed paint. There were no curtains at the windows, only drawn shades. Pete's old Chevy wagon was in the yard.

I parked on the street, and got out. A police patrol car drove slowly by. A white face leaned out its window.

"You!"

I stopped. The policeman got out of the car.

"You got some business here, mister?"

"Why?" I said.

"Don't be smart. You got identification?"

I produced my driver's license and a courtesy card from the New York Police. He reddened.

"Sorry, Mr. Shaw. This is a bad area. Just our job."

He went back to the patrol car, drove off. I walked on across the yard and up the shabby porch. The door opened before I knocked. Pete Wallace stood there. He looked past me toward the disappearing police car.

"The mothers! That's what we live with, Paul. You just walk, and they stop you. Come on in. Any word, man?"

He still wore his black leather jacket, his beret, and his dark glasses. It was a uniform, he wore it with pride. He needed pride in something. The living room of the tiny house had holes in the plaster walls, splintered floorboards, and a rain-stained ceiling. The furniture was sagging and broken. Wallpaper peeled. The remains of food were scattered around. Through the open bedroom door I saw an unmade bed and more peeling wallpaper. Pete had probably lived in worse places in his orphan days.

"No word," I said. "You?"

"Not a whisper," he said. He brushed some clothes from a stained chair. "Sit down, man. I'd have fixed the joint up some, only the roof leaks and rats come in from the quarry. Things'll get better."

"I want to talk to John Morgan, Pete," I said.

"Okay. What's Johnny got to do with it?"

"I know Judy came here the day she vanished," I said. "She was here the next day, called from here that night.

She had two appointments in L.A. She never showed. Either two people lied to me, or she changed her plans, or she never left here."

He sat down. John Morgan was his leader, and fighting breeds loyalty.

"If Johnny lied, he could have a lot of reasons," he said. "He takes Malcolm X's words real serious."

"'Those who say don't know; those who know don't say?'"

"Like that," Pete said. "Morgan's a strange cat, Paul. A lot of times I feel he's all on his own. He had a bad life, in and out of jail. Rape, assault, all that. Sometimes—" His eyes flickered behind the dark glasses. "We're all in the Movement together, any one of us is dead tomorrow. Johnny Morgan's a good leader, only . . . sometimes I get the idea he's out for himself too much."

"Is he violent? Not for the cause, for himself?"

"Why, Paul?"

I was on slippery ground. He was a Panther. If the Panthers were behind it all, he wasn't going to tell me, whether he knew anything or not. I had a hunch that John Morgan wouldn't tell him much, knowing Pete knew me, but I couldn't be sure.

"I was wondering if he'd act on his own," I said.

"He maybe would."

"Does he want to build a reputation?"

"Our chapter's small, he likes power, yeh."

"Did he like Judy? Want her, maybe?"

He studied the broken floor. "Maybe. Morgan's funny with women. Smooth and easy, treats them nice, acts soft. I never believed it. Women he just uses, even his wife."

"He used Judy, Pete?"

"I don't know," he said, looked up, the dark glasses reflecting sunlight. "I'll level, Paul. Morgan's been kind of uptight. We've had some raids, one bad one only two weeks ago. It's got us all edgy, but Morgan the most."

"I've got to see him, Pete."

He thought about it. "Step soft, you know?"

"I'm carrying a gun," I said.

"Where is it?"

"Shoulder holster."

"Okay, you told me."

He went into his bedroom to make his telephone call.

26 ᕈ

I HEARD THE CAR drive up. An old blue Ford. They got out and hurried into the house. There were four of them: John Morgan, a woman, and two other men in berets and leather jackets. They came in carefully, checked the bedroom, and the two I didn't know took up posts at the front windows. The woman stayed with John Morgan.

"You want to talk to me, Shaw?" Morgan said.

He didn't introduce the woman. He was bigger than I had realized, his large Arab nose stronger. Maybe it was the black leather jacket and beret he wore now, the uniform. The woman was young and slender, pale-skinned and cold-eyed. She didn't like me there.

Pete Wallace said, "Judy's an old friend of Paul's, Johnny. He's worried. Carlos hired him. Two weeks, you know?"

Morgan nodded. "You find any leads on Judy, or maybe on who beat up Carlos?"

"Judy called a man in L.A.," I said. "The day after she vanished. She was here. She said she'd seen you and she was calling from your headquarters."

"She's a liar!" the young woman snapped. "It's another try to frame us, Johnny. Let's run this honky out!"

"Slow, Mama," Morgan said. He smiled. "My wife's a real blood, Shaw. Tougher than any of us. Make you nervous?"

"Yes," I said, "she makes me nervous. I got caught by the Cong once in Viet Nam. I was nervous then."

"Caught by our yellow brothers? How'd you get out?"

"I ran," I said. "They made a mistake."

"We made a bigger going there," Morgan said.

I said, "I can agree on that."

His tragic face seemed to be seeing that mountain he lived to climb. "Only thirty million of them to start, but they beat the Japs, kicked out the French, and they're beating the Americans. That's what we have to make our people understand—we can do it. Sure, all out, America could beat them, but it can't be all out. The racists can't go all out here, right? Counting all color minorities, there's thirty million of us."

"Revolution?" I said. "You think it's possible?"

He rubbed at his nose. "Not now. Our people have to learn how to fight, get allies. That's our job—to teach them. Riots help, even if they're bad tactics. You learn to fight by fighting. Then you need a revolutionist cadre, and an enemy you can see easy. We've got our enemy, our occupying army—the police in the ghettos. Look in the eyes of any boy in the ghetto, Shaw, you'll see them look at the cops the same way French Resistance fighters looked at German soldiers. All they need is leaders and a program. We're the program, that's why the cops want to wipe us out any way they can."

"And the leaders, too?" I said.

"Those of us who stay alive," Morgan said.

Morgan's wife said, "No more prayin' and boot-licking. You know, honky, I had a brother. Fifteen. He busted into a store because we were hungry. The cops caught him. He was wrong, sure, he should of gone to reform school. We found him with ten shotgun pellets in him. 'Trying to escape.' A fifteen-year-old boy, unarmed, and they couldn't stop him any other way? He was real dangerous, like all niggers, right? If he'd been a white boy he'd be in jail—not dead!"

"Someday we'll all resist," Morgan said, "and then they'll slaughter us. When that happens, even dudes like Whitney Young come with us. We have to awaken our people politically, so we're ready. It's not so hard to die for a cause, it's harder to live, work, and kill for it."

I said, "Are you telling me about necessary violence?"

Pete Wallace said, "Violence is what the honkies know. Everybody's afraid of a gun, a knife."

"Let's all bury our guns," Morgan said. "The cops, too. Then no black man'll have to live in fear, and no white man. We hate violence, I mean that. But it's not violent to shoot a cop who busts into your home to kill you. It's a man's right to defend his home—any man, black or white. When anyone busts into your house, civilian or cop, you put a gun in his face, and you say, 'Split, you mother!' If he don't split—"

"The police have to enforce law, Morgan. If they come with a warrant—"

"No!" Morgan said. "We've had too many brothers killed in ghettos all over for 'resisting,' 'escaping,' and for no reason at all, like in Detroit. We can't trust. They want to make an arrest, they stand outside with their warrants!"

"Shoot back is the only answer?" I said.

Morgan sighed. "We can call the U.N. and protest. Get hold of the Civil Liberties Union. Petition the Supreme Court. Maybe call the police station— Hey, come stop these cops from shootin' us up! Do any of that, then wait. If you're not dead by then."

One of the men at the windows said, "I was a big athlete in high school, with white boys. When I got to be twenty-three I was a laborer scratching to support a wife and kids. Twice I got jived for standing on my own block. When I found an outfit that don't walk around singing hymns, I joined. No more talking and praying and waiting for the saints to march down and free us. That's the jive Whitey conned us with for three hundred years. No more."

They had a cause, and they lived it, and breathed it. What did I tell them? That I thought they were wrong? That they had to be more objective, and I had to be? It's hard for a victim to be objective. Did I tell them that I had my work, that my only interest in their revolution now was what it might have done to Judy? No matter how much a man believed in a cause, he was still a man, and my job was with the hidden corners.

"You want to help people, Morgan," I said. "I'm trying to help a girl we both know. I want to find her. I know you saw her that Tuesday. If you, or your cause, haven't done anything to her, you'll tell me what you know. I'm no enemy."

His dark face was immobile. He thought about it all without haste. "I saw Judy that day, yeh. In Dave Eigen's apartment, where I met you. Around two P.M. She asked me to lay off Frank Carlos, let him quit the Movement. That's it."

"What did you say?"

"I said no," Morgan said. "We need every brother, a man like Frank Carlos especially. He's Puerto Rican and a name, he can bring the young cats into the party. Then I left her with Dave Eigen."

"She came to your headquarters later?"

"No."

"Why would she say she was there?"

"I wouldn't know, man."

"Someone's lying. Why would Judy lie about it then?"

The hush in the room was heavy enough to crush a man. Morgan's wife looked like she would hit me herself. She was an enemy I wouldn't have liked to face in a strange place. Not that I would want to face John Morgan. He breathed hard.

"You got hormones, man," he said softly. "I like that, I'm a Yankee Doodle cat, after all. Trouble is, the Zulus were bloods who saluted the guts of their enemies, and they lost. We figure to win, and a man don't fool with the golden rule in a crowd that don't play fair. You just remember that."

He walked out like the guerrilla general he was, his wife and troops peeling out of the room behind him, fast and alert. I didn't move until I heard the car start, and pull away. I felt like the enemy. I didn't like that feeling. Not one bit.

27 ~

I DIDN'T WANT to be their enemy. I didn't want to be the enemy of anything except the evil of this world, and they weren't that, whatever they did. Or whatever they had done. I looked at Pete Wallace.

"Well?" I said.

"I don't know, man. Johnny's uptight, so is Felicia."

"Felicia? That's her name, Morgan's wife? She wouldn't like any woman Morgan played with, would she?"

"No, she wouldn't." He was uneasy now.

I said, "Are the Panthers against Judy, Pete?"

"Not so far as they told me. That's straight jive," he said. "Only . . . they know Judy and me are old friends, Paul, you know? They know I worked with her close in our ghetto theater, and down with Mr. Max. Maybe they don't tell me."

No, maybe they wouldn't tell Pete. On the other hand, I had only Rick Elliot's word about when Judy called, and where she called from. Elliot had a good reason to place her in San Perdido at 8:00 P.M., and maybe to hint she hadn't been alone.

"Let's see what Dave Eigen has to say now," I said.

Pete nodded. "Yeh, I'll go along, okay?"

"I'll try to get Eigen working against Morgan," I said.

"Morgan ain't taking us nowhere," he said.

"You wouldn't want to keep an eye on me, would you, Pete?" I said. He didn't answer. "Okay, I'll respect your commitment to your brothers, but don't fight me. Fair?"

"Yeh, Paul, that's fair."

We took my car to drive up Fremont Street to Dave Eigen's apartment. He wasn't there. We went back to the car and drove to the campus. Eigen wasn't in his office, either, but it wasn't empty. Dr. Jonas Eyk was there, with a student.

"Have you found Judith, Mr. Shaw?" Eyk said.

"No. Where's Dave Eigen?"

"At the demonstration."

"What demonstration?"

Eyk sat on a desk, swung his leg. "The administration has banned the scheduled appearance of a radical professor, one William Allen. Last month George Wallace was allowed to speak—with words from the governor about free speech. It does make one wonder." Eyk's mouth was set in a thin, hard line. "The mood this year is one of silence, but if the authorities think this means problems are over, they need a fresh look. The action is merely underground. Force rarely makes converts, it makes guerrillas."

The student spoke up. He was a neat boy, dressed in an older campus style I knew from my day.

"I'm a kid," he said, "but the strike last year taught me

how the authorities argue against change. Their arguments are force and repression. Bayonets and spies. It makes me wonder if they have any arguments. I didn't support the strike, but I've been listening to Dave Eigen. I don't want Dave telling me what to do and I don't want the Panthers. But I know the Panthers tell the truth when they say what's *wrong*. I want my leaders to make it better, not tell me how good it all is when I can *see* it's not so good."

"Yes," I said. "Where is this demonstration?"

"At the City Hall," Eyk said. "Shaw, I've been thinking about Judith. She's an outspoken girl, and I know how she thinks. The city and campus are in an ugly mood underneath. An atmosphere of struggle breeds all kinds of lunatics. Judy is naïve, too honest. You know her, Wallace."

Pete leaned on a wall. "She cuts people down, yeh."

Eyk said, "She told the sheriff to his face that he feared change more than the students feared him. He didn't like it."

The young student said, "We're on campus to learn. The sheriff, and the governor, don't seem to want that. They know what they think of Professor Allen. I haven't heard him. They don't want me to hear him, they want me to believe them, not think. Indoctrination, just like Russia, not education. I'm only twenty, I want to listen to my country, but I want to hear more than 'Believe, sonny, and do as you're told.' You know?"

Pete Wallace watched the student like a tiger watching a lamb. "You get nowhere unless you scare them, man. No one listens. No one even sees you."

"I don't want to scare anyone," the student said.

Eyk said, "Judy told me once that I was to blame for all the trouble. I was furious, I knew she was right. We middle-aged liberals who should have created the new programs for change became technicians of facts and past ideas, were kept busy by corporate and state money. Now there are no real programs for change. We failed in the forties and fifties to develop ideas, we left the world to the Reagans. Now the kids are full of frustrations, with no solutions because we didn't teach them any. Judy said I was, and had, nothing."

I could hear her voice. That blunt voice impatient with untruth and mediocrity: *"I'm Judy Tower. I've watched you in class. You're not good . . . No lies, Paul, no lies."* The ambitious and committed prefer lies that say what they want to hear.

"You think she got involved in a fight?" I said.

"She was disturbed, Shaw, she never had any caution."

"No," I said. "She never did. Not any way."

Eyk let that pass, and we left the office. As we went to my car, I thought about Dr. Jonas Eyk. He had talked a lot about politics and trouble. Maybe to cover a different lack of caution on Judy's part? *Fakes . . . behind nice, smooth fronts,* Judy had said to Rick Elliot. Some rotten scripts.

"Does Dr. Eyk write plays, Pete? Scripts?"

"Maybe, I think yeh. Judy said something when we worked in the ghetto. Professor of Speech and all, man."

"Does anyone else write up here?"

"Not that I heard, Paul."

I thought more about Jonas Eyk as we drove to City Hall. I heard the noise of a crowd before we got there. The streets were cordoned off, we had to walk the last two blocks. The open square was jammed with young people. We pushed through to the speakers' platform. David Eigen was up there, but he wasn't speaking yet. A series of speakers talked about the right to listen and decide. The crowd cheered them. Then Eigen got up. His skinny body seemed ten inches taller. He leaned on the rostrum. His voice was clear and resonant:

"They won't let us hear. Last year we struck, and lost. Maybe it's time again." His tone was quiet, as if reading the contents of a new college course. "Strike to hear. Strike against argument by cops. Strike to control your own lives. Strike because they give us no poetry in their lectures. Strike because their facts lie. Strike to live. Strike!"

The crowd took it up, the single word over and over: *Strike! Strike! Strike!* I saw the police. They were coming out of the side streets: city policemen; sheriff's deputies; highway patrolmen; and some National Guardsmen. Hurrying. In full riot gear. The students were still watching David Eigen, hadn't even seen the police yet. Screams were just starting on the edges.

I said to Pete Wallace, "Let's get out of here."

"Hey, man," he said softly, a smile on his face that was almost joyful. "They was waiting, all ready! You don't get all those cats in a hurry. They got it planned. Stop the kids fast and hard."

"They'll love you," I said.

"I hear you, let's split."

We walked away. Out of the crowd and quickly down a side street. The police were all hurrying toward the square, took no notice of us. We didn't run, we walked easily to the next main avenue. On the corners passers-by stopped to watch the action a block away on the square; other people walked on about their business. Groups of students had followed our example, simply walked away from the square.

"We'll go back and wait for Eigen at his place," I said.

"If he don't get busted, Paul," Pete said.

"There wasn't any trouble. The cops got there before anything happened."

I saw the squad of sheriff's deputies and city policemen approach. They reached where Pete and I stood with a group of city people and students.

A sheriff's captain pointed at us. "Get those, all of 'em."

They surrounded us. Pete tried to run. A deputy hit him with a nightstick. Pete was down. I moved toward him. Two policemen grabbed me, handcuffed me to a man who was protesting that he was a doctor on a call. A policeman slapped the man. The other policeman looked at me as if daring me to resist.

"Am I under arrest?" I said.

"You sure are, buddy."

"What charge?"

"Paradin' without a permit."

"I wasn't parading, I was standing—a block away."

The sheriff's captain came by. "Shut him up! You hear me, shut up! No talking! No one talks from here on!"

Handcuffed, we waited. I saw a bewildered man in a city Water Department uniform looking down at the handcuffs that chained him to a long-haired girl in a poncho. The cops stood around us, grinning.

"Now you gonna get it, hippies!"

"Real tough revolutionaries, yessir!"

"You got no rocks to throw now, you punks?"

All around, people stood and watched, some of them students. The police paid no attention to them. A random bust. I could see policemen still arresting people—mostly young people. A paddy wagon rolled up. We were all pushed in. I tried to identify myself to the captain.

"Captain? Listen, I'm a priv—"

"Shut up! You hear?" He glared at me.

No one had a chance to identify himself. We were pushed into the wagon—all shapes, colors, sizes, and ages. There was even a Good Humor man in his white suit.

As we rolled away I looked for Pete Wallace. I couldn't see him. Instead I saw a gang of deputies pushing another group out of the side street toward another wagon. One of the prisoners was David Eigen. A deputy had him by his long hair.

28 🪶

"OKAY, OUT! Everybody out—fast!"

We stumbled out in single file.

"No talking, march, or you get a stick in the mouth!"

Two students were hit and knocked down. Guards dragged them up. I looked around and saw four big, square brick buildings behind a high barbed-wire fence. There were prison towers. It looked like a small Alcatraz, maximum security. We were marched inside.

"Sit down! Against the wall! Knees up to chins! Now!"

We sat. My knees up to my chin stretched the stitches in my side. My shoulder had begun to throb again. All down the line of men, guards were clubbing anyone whose feet moved, whose heads turned right or left.

"No moving, eyes front!"

Two hours passed. The guards dragged man after man out of the seated line, made them kneel, and beat them with clubs. The guards were like wild animals out of control, maddened. They roamed up and down the lines of men, clubbing ankles, smashing any hand that moved.

"Junkies! . . . Filthy beatniks! . . . Damned Commies . . ."

"You're gonna learn a lesson, yessir!"

"No more trouble from you people!"

Another hour, and it was growing dark. My side was bleeding again now, my shoulder hammering from the cramped position, my legs numb. I made no protest; I had been caught by the Viet Cong once, I knew that nothing would stop them the way they were now. Silence was the defense, call no attention. But my mind was busy.

They had cracked, the police and guards. They must have been told that we were all rioters. They hated us. I counted close to four hundred prisoners all around the yard of the prison. An indiscriminate bust, stupid and in panic, and now the guards were out of their minds with hate. What had Dr. Eyk said—the atmosphere is revolutionary, such an atmosphere breeds all kinds of fringe lunatics. It also breeds lunatics in the heart of the land—these guards and police were not on the fringe.

"I count three, everybody up!"

Those who were slow were clubbed, kicked, punched.

"Inside! Single file. Double time! Now! Hut—hut—hut!"

There were too many of us to book, to even search, at once. We double-timed into the cold building and a large holding tank cell. They left the doors open, stood in rows outside, with clubs held in both hands, watching us. I had seen it like that before—in Viet Nam, our guards standing like that in front of groups of squatting Viet Cong prisoners. Only in Viet Nam they held guns not clubs. The Viet Cong guards were different—when they held us, we stood and they squatted, watching for a chance to club us, or kill us.

"Everybody sit! No moving. No talking!"

More hours. It was cold in the unheated tank. From time to time the guards charged into us, clubbing someone who had moved, or just someone they decided to enjoy clubbing. They were defeating their own commands—purposely— making the place a bedlam of yelling, moving, screams of pain. They dragged men out in groups of three and four, kicked them toward a desk where a captain finally booked them. One desk.

I saw Dave Eigen.

He was far in the rear of the tank, huddled in a corner. It was all so mindless, they hadn't even identified leaders. But they would, if there was any order left at all, and I wanted Eigen. I began to work my way back, sitting down. These guards weren't even competent. I had escaped the Viet

Cong, and the Cong were competent. It was dark in the rear corner.

"Eigen!"

He jerked as if kicked. "What?"

"It's Paul Shaw," I hissed, my face close to his.

He winced, scared. "Shaw? I—"

"You lied about Judy," I whispered. "You saw her."

"No!"

"Morgan told me. Where is she, Eigen?"

His eyes darted everywhere, searching for escape. If he moved, the guards would beat him. A call for help wouldn't be listened to. His face was already bloody with cuts, bruises, missing teeth.

I put my face inches from his. I felt his rapid, frightened breathing. I whispered, harshly, "Eigen, I've been in places like this. I can break your arm here, and not be caught. Cripple you, or kill you, and no one the wiser. Eigen, tell me about Judy."

"I . . . I don't know . . ."

I clamped my hand over his mouth, and hit him in the stomach. I felt the insanity of the guards in me. I'd been beaten, I was bleeding, my shoulder hammered. A schizophrenia was part of the day, the place, of me now. I wanted Judy! His eyes bulged at me like the eyes of a terrified rabbit.

I took my hand away. "Eigen? You saw her that day."

He nodded, beaten, his whisper low. "The afternoon. Morgan was there. She wanted us to tell Frank Carlos we didn't need him. Morgan refused, and left. I . . . I said I would tell Carlos we didn't want him back if . . . I tried to make love to her. She slapped me. She left."

"Where did she go?"

"I don't know."

"That's not enough to make you lie to me. Eigen?"

He licked his lips. They were bone-dry and cracked with fear. He was trying to stand up to the guards and to me. We were too much together, and I had to know. I held his arm.

"No!" His voice too loud, his eyes jumping toward the guards. They hadn't heard. I balled my fist. He gave up.

"The Panthers think she's a spy," he whispered, so low I almost missed it. "There was a raid a few days later. The cops knew too much. They told me Judy could be a spy."

"A spy? Judy? For who?"

"I don't know! Maybe because she wanted Carlos out. They had spies close before—wives, brothers, friends."

"What did they do to her, Eigen?"

"Nothing! They wouldn't do—"

"Then where is she?"

"I don't know!" He cringed, and then there was a light in his scared eyes. "The cabin! Maybe the cabin. She said she'd maybe go there. A cabin in the Sierras, near Perdido."

"A cabin? Who with?"

"She didn't say anything about that. The cabin belongs to her boss in L.A., a guy named Tarra. She said she wanted to go there soon, get away from it all, just work. She hoped she could go there real soon. Maybe she went!"

"Did John Morgan know about the cabin?"

"I don't know. I don't know who she talked to after she left me. She—"

His rabbit eyes bulged. I looked. A guard had spotted us. He charged through the pack of huddled prisoners. I rolled away to the darkest part of the cell. The guard saw me escaping, ignored Eigen, came down on me with his club high. I went in under the club, hit him in the groin, butted him hard in the stomach. He yelled. I hit him in the face with a hard right. He went over. I dropped with him in the dark. I crawled in among the prisoners, many standing now out of reflex—kids and plain citizens. I crawled, snaked, and reached a wall, where I sat against it with my knees up, head down, proper.

Five guards charged to their fallen comrade. They clubbed everyone near—the guilty had to be one of the nearest, right? I felt more than sick—at the guards, at the day, at the sounds of beating, at myself. Sick at what I'd done to Dave Eigen, at the pain I caused others because I had to be a "man" and hit that guard, at my own skill in evading where others had no skill. But—Judy, a spy?

They helped the fallen guard out, and calm slowly settled again. Another hour passed, or hours, I didn't know. Judy, a spy? No. But if John Morgan, or anyone, thought—? Then there was the cabin. Had she gone to the Sierra cabin? Tarra's cabin? Emil Tarra, who hadn't wanted to tell me anything at all, and who would know Gloria Kazko? I had to get out of this insane nightmare. Somehow. When they booked me, yes.

They got to me just before midnight. The second of four men. I stepped up to the table out in the wide corridor of the cell block. The captain didn't even look up. He held his hand out while he wrote the last entry for the man before me.

"Wallet and papers," he said.

I gave them to him. "Captain, I'm a priv—"

An arm went around my throat. Hands held my arms. A hand reached in under my coat.

"This one's got a gun!"

The gun was in the hand of an incredulous deputy. The guards stood frozen. The captain looked at the gun. His face was white. He was thinking about what could have happened to him because his guards had failed to search the prisoners. He licked his lips, looked up at me.

"This is real bad trouble, mister," he said.

"No," I said, "I've got a permit. Look in my wallet."

He looked through my wallet. Time seemed to stand still in that dim, cold corridor. He closed my wallet. Sat back.

"What job are you doing, Shaw?" he said.

"Nothing you're part of. You made a mistake, Captain."

He fingered my wallet, touched my gun, which was on the table now. "I'll have to think. Put him away by himself,

Sergeant. Five in block two is empty."

"I get a call, Captain."

"No you don't," he said.

They marched me across the yard, where kids, clerks, and shopgirls were still being clubbed to sit against the walls. The cell they put me in was small and dark. There was nothing to do now but sleep. I needed sleep.

Tomorrow I'd find a way out—maybe.

29 ᕈᙡᕈ

I woke up, stiff and sore. Dawn light filtered in through the bars of the single window in the cell. I was alone. All through the cell block men were coughing, hawking, and laughing. It was a regular cell block, criminal prisoners. I went to the window. It overlooked the prison yard.

Hundreds of people were out there—all kneeling in narrow lines. They were, in the dawn light, people you would see on any street in a college town. Kids everywhere, mostly with long hair and beards and college clothes, but not all. Young and middle-aged men in business suits—bloody, crumpled, torn. Girls and women in a group by themselves. I saw the Water Department man kneeling with the rest. I didn't see the Good Humor man, or Dave Eigen, but I could have missed Maureen in the mob out there.

I went away from the window, and sat on the bunk. They were feeding the prisoners, it would take a long time. I wondered if any of them had gotten to make telephone calls to relatives or lawyers. I hadn't seen anyone make a call last night. There must have been almost five hundred, indiscriminately arrested, having committed no crimes, humiliated, beaten, allowed no calls, not even allowed to identify themselves, bloody and jailed. In America.

After another hour I heard the shouting in unison and the sound of men marching—army sounds I still hated. I went back to the window. The guards were having a ball. The prisoners were double-timing up and down the yard, shouting: "WE LOVE THE MEAN COPS! . . . WE LOVE THE MEAN COPS! . . ."

Bloody, sleepless, and terrorized, the civilians, young and old, stumbled and bumped into each other. The guards clubbed them, then roared with laughter. I looked toward the main gate. No one and nothing was coming into the prison. How long could they keep the lawyers and relatives away? Five hundred random citizens had a lot of relatives. This was still America.

A silent deputy brought my breakfast. He left.

No one else came near me. Then I heard a low, rising hum of excitement out in the yard. I went to the window. The main gate was open. Cars drove in, and civilians with briefcases got out. They walked angry. Lawyers. I watched the guards spit on the ground—damned lawyers come to coddle the dirty criminal anarchists. My watch said it was twenty hours.

No one came for me.

Maureen and Dick Delaney would be wondering by now, but I hadn't called to tell them where I was. They knew I was in San Perdido. Delaney would start looking, but he wouldn't think of a police sweep. After all, this was Delaney's home. This was California. It didn't happen here.

At 5:00 P.M. a small San Perdido city policeman came in with my dinner. I was hungry. The policeman didn't leave.

"You Shaw?"

"I think so," I said. "I think I'm in California, too."

"The captain, he was a colonel in Viet Nam."

"Which side?" I said.

"Yeh," he said. "Look, I don't like this. They're short of men, they asked us to help out. It ain't going to make my job easier from here on. I got to try to police the city."

"Maybe you better police the sheriff first."

He was silent. Then, "They're scared of you. They think maybe you're watching them, a shoo-fly."

I sat up. "They think I'm a spy-cop?"

"They're not letting you out, or near a phone. They're trying to check on you, quiet like."

I was scared. Alone, unarmed, in the captain's prison that was emptying rapidly. They were dumb enough to think they might beat the charges of five hundred private citizens, gloss it over cop to cop. But they weren't dumb enough to think they could evade the report of a cop sent to report on them.

"Can you get word out? One of your bosses?" I said. "Wait! There's a Lieutenant Devine. Tell him, fast."

"Pat Devine? Okay. But I'm not off before midnight."

It was the best I could do. It wasn't very good. Alone, I lay awake and thinking—about myself now. I had seen a lot of jails and prisons. I knew the way "accidents" could happen, and how fatal they could be. Dead, I'd be a small stink, like those dead prisoners on Arkansas prison farms. Alive, I could tell, and maybe be a very big stink.

I jumped at every footstep in the corridor.

By midnight I began to wonder if I was on the same earth.

I slept.

I woke up to the sun again.

Prison happens fast to a man. I found that I already had to think about what day it was.

Saturday. I had been held since Thursday afternoon.

A guard came with breakfast. He watched me with nervous eyes. I wasn't hungry by now.

I watched the prison yard all morning.

My fellow civilians still drifted out the gate in twos and

threes. It took time to get rid of five hundred angry men. The guards stood sullen, stared hate at every prisoner who walked out that gate. Hate and fear. The orgy was over, and now the guards stood like men with a Sunday-morning hangover. Shaky in the morning-after light, not wishing that they hadn't done it, but only that no one would tell.

No lunch was brought.

The sun moved down the sky beyond my barred window. The guards stood in small groups in the yard. Every prisoner who trickled out that gate was another nail in their coffin—the burial of their jobs. A few of them. Those few would feel bad for a week or two, and then would find other work. Their work would change, but not their hate. They would hate more. The cause of all their troubles would be the dirty prisoners, the beatnik bums! *They* would be to blame, the damned weirdos!

The guard who brought a sandwich for my dinner didn't look at me.

I lay awake in the dark of another night.

The terror of prison is the helplessness. Anything can be done to you—anything.

A change came over my mind. For two days I had watched the door for help to come through. I had waited for it to open. Now I only wanted it to never open. Now I watched the door for harm to come through.

The closed door that had been my enemy was now my friend. Let it stay closed, let no one come to hurt me.

I was a prisoner. I knew now.

I slept again.

There was sun at the barred window when I opened my eyes this time. Late. I didn't think about that. I heard what had awakened me—footsteps in the corridor, at my door.

The door opened. A prison sergeant I had seen before with a club in his hand came in. He had my gun in his hand now.

My own gun.

30 ⌒

THE SERGEANT TOOK two steps into the cell. I stood up.

Lieutenant Patrick Devine came in behind the sergeant. His tall frame seemed stooped under some weight. His red hair was hatless, his freckled face set. His voice rasped: "Give them to him."

The sergeant held out my gun, holster, and wallet. I took them, holstered the gun. The sergeant's eyes were flat.

"Now get down with the captain," Devine said.

The sergeant left the cell.

Devine looked at me. "Supervisors are downstairs," he said. "You want to make a speech and feel good, or you want to get the hell out of here?"

"Let's get out," I said.

He took me down a back staircase and out to his dusty car. Two minutes later we were on our way to San Perdido. I didn't look back at the barbed wire and cell blocks.

"I was away," Devine said. "The patrolman didn't want to talk to the wrong man. The sheriff has friends in our department. I called your partner, Delaney. He's told your wife you're okay. You can file a full complaint at headquarters."

"No," I said, "they don't need my complaint."

He kept his eyes on the road. "I want to get them all, Shaw. I want to stay a cop, and feel good about it."

I had known that the time would come when the police would catch up to me. It looked like this was a good time to let them. I had a weapon, my three days in prison. I could deal from strength.

"I'd have to tell about what I'm doing here," I said. "My hands aren't clean, Devine."

"The Frank Carlos case?" he said.

"You found out? My cover story didn't hold?"

"Your story held," Devine said, "except we found no trace of prowlers operating in Gloria Kazko's area, and her background was all soap and ribbons—except for The Carleton Club. I got to thinking about that club, and a kind of bell rang. I thought I'd heard the name recently. So I nosed around in recent cases, and came up with L.A.'s teletype to us about Frank Carlos. I saw that Carlos' wife was missing, and she worked at The Carleton Club. I remembered you coming from L.A. to talk to Gloria Kazko."

"Did you follow up on it in L.A.?"

"A little, but I didn't mention you. I wanted to hear what you had to say first. Why'd you lie?"

I told him the whole story of the case. He listened as he drove, and we were in San Perdido now. It looked all calm, quiet, and the same. That surprised me. In jail I had imagined the streets in chaos, debris everywhere. Devine didn't look at the streets. He was thinking about what I had told him.

"This Judy Carlos is an old girl friend of yours? You figured she was maybe in danger, or maybe had tried to get Frank Carlos killed herself?"

"Let's say I wanted to reach her first, and hear her side," I said. "I didn't like Captain Watts down in L.A."

"Watts is a good commander, but narrow," Devine said. "How the hell do we make cops broader and more objective than the average man they serve? Make them control trouble, not be part of it, or even make it." He glowered at a traffic light that held us up. His freckled face was made to be a happy face, but he was a serious man. "Okay, we owe you one mistake, maybe two. Officially, you reported to me all along."

"Thanks," I said. "Now tell me about the case."

He smiled at last. I hadn't fooled him. He knew I'd known he had to react that way after my three days.

"I'll check on the latest reports, you go see our Doc."

He pulled into the parking lot of the courthouse. It was a beautiful Spanish-Moorish building on the same square where my trouble had started. The square was empty now.

"Your car is over there," Devine said. "It was ticketed and towed away. Your bag's in it. We'll forget the tickets."

The police doctor changed my bandages and said I was okay. I got my bag from the car and changed in the police locker room. I took my first shower in three days, and I could have slept a month. I thought about Judy instead, about the "atmosphere" around San Perdido, and what it had done to me. I went up to Devine's office to wait. He showed up at noon.

"Lunch on the city," he said. "Last reparation, okay?"

The restaurant was a good steak house with trimmings. Devine was on duty, but we both had whiskies. It looked like today he didn't give a damn. With the food, he got down to business.

"L.A. talked to everyone you did except Elliot, plus some fringe people. No one has seen Judy Carlos since the Monday, they say, so you're ahead of them. I went on a limb, didn't tell them about you or Elliot. You'll do better alone for now."

"I've lost three days," I said.

"Yeh," he said. "Most of those guards are young guys back from Viet Nam. They think protesters should be treated like Viet Cong. They serve order, and that means a kind of military order: obey all rules, stay in line, never question."

"The kids and blacks make them flip?"

"Not just them. A lot of my own men arrest a bearded kid for walking on the grass, turn loose a businessman they *saw* try to molest a girl. But guards and cops don't act like that unless their bosses think like that. Our sheriff makes speeches about shooting anyone running from a fire."

"Just the man to reform what happened," I said.

He drank. "Charges dropped, except a few on leaders to prove there was cause for the arrests. Seven men suspended at the prison, including the captain. He says he'll be sheriff."

"He probably will be," I said. I pushed my plate away. "Except a few hundred people came out of that prison ready to listen to Eigen and John Morgan now. Stupid! Prisons and force never changed one man's mind if he really believed, but they make a believer out of a neutral every time."

Devine signaled for coffee. "You know what a police state is, Shaw? It's not cops ruling, it's when the powerful and the respectable use the police to keep things the way they want them. The cop is a tool. If we don't think hard, we'll have a police state in ten years or less. I'm a cop because I like the feel of protecting people, helping them. I don't want to be a kind of concentration-camp guard for one group."

What did I say? The times were squeezing Devine, and all like him, harder than anyone. He had a job that was souring around him. When the coffee came, I lit a cigarette.

"You have to enforce the laws, Devine," I said.

He stirred his coffee, sadly. "You know, people like the Panthers are trying to enforce laws—the laws of equal rights. They're trying to change bad laws, too—the social laws that always work against the poor. But they've pretty near given up on law too." He drank some coffee. "I'm a cop, I hope the 'rule of law' will work someday, but it never has. No one has ever accepted a law against their real gut interests. For over a hundred years, Shaw, the majority of America has refused to obey the law of the Thirteenth and Fourteenth Amendments—they just don't want blacks equal! Now the minorities are rebelling for their gut passions, and there's no law in rebellion. It's stupid to think there could be."

I had no answer. I wondered if anyone did.

Devine said, "No society ever permits revolution, no rebel

asks permission to rebel, damn it. Laws about rebellion just maintain the status quo. You stop rebellion just two ways: by removing the cause, or by force. You give the rebels what they need, or you control them by force, period."

"No compromise, Devine?"

"Hell, compromise means give the rebels as little as possible, try to break their ranks. It has to be backed by force, and rebels know it for what it is. Rebels use compromise as a time to gather strength for another attack, and the state knows that. Compromise got about as much value as the sheriff yelling about criminals and outside agitators. Criminals try to use all rebellions, and no revolution works without agitators. You talk about outside agitators, all you're saying is you had your downtrodden under nice control, and laws never stopped agitators."

He pushed his coffee cup away, slopping it over the table. "You know what the trouble really is today? We majority whites don't want order, we want to keep our advantages. We're hanging onto our privileges, period. What *we* have that *they* don't have. All talk about reason, law, and order just means keeping everything to the advantage of the white majority. As long as that's the way it is, we'll have to rule by force and nothing else."

"You make it sound hopeless," I said.

"Maybe it is," he said. "Injustice or disorder, tyranny or chaos. It depends who you are. The man who loses by chaos prefers tyranny. The victims of injustice prefer disorder. If you want both order and real justice, you climb a tree."

His voice had become loud, and people were looking at us. Mostly businessmen. Some of them must have known Devine, who he was. They didn't look pleased. I wondered how long he'd keep his job? I didn't think he'd care much, and my mind was on Judy again. Devine talked of violence, force, and conflict, and Judy was out there somewhere.

"The atmosphere of violence," I said. "Judy Carlos is gone three weeks now. Caught in the grind? Gone crazy?

Run away from it all? I've got lies, cloak-and-dagger, and a possible love nest. Maybe none of that at all."

"You do what you can, try to find her," Devine said.

"Where are all my people?"

"Dave Eigen and Pete Wallace were held. Eigen was a speaker, Wallace is a Panther. They got out today. Dr. Eyk's at home."

"John Morgan?"

"He's missing, Shaw, so's his wife."

"Missing? From where?"

"Everywhere," Devine said. "We pulled a raid on Panther headquarters yesterday. On a tip. We got some more illegal guns, but Morgan and his wife weren't there."

"A tip?" I said. "Who from?"

He just sat.

I said, "Devine, maybe the Panthers think Judy's a spy. You made a raid two weeks ago, now another. A tip from a woman?"

"No," he said.

"Okay, but the tipster could be a key. I want him."

His face was blank, I was pushing him. "All right. A small-time private detective named Perry Lint. A nasty item. Lives in the ghetto on a banana peel. Buys and sells information, mostly with fear. A hustler for any dollar he can find. He scares even me sometimes."

"He tipped you both times?"

"Yeh," he said. "I'm trusting you a long way. Don't let me down, and don't put me in a bind."

"I won't, Lieutenant. Where do I find Lint?"

He shook his head. "Lint works out of his shoes. I'll arrange a meet, point him out. Let's go."

From Devine's office I called Maureen and Delaney. Delaney had nothing for me, Maureen cried. She had thought I was hurt.

"Only my pride and faith," I said. "How are you, baby?"

"They say I can go home in a day or so. When will you be here? I don't want to be alone, Paul."

"Soon, baby. Stay close to Delaney."

"All right, darling. Please be careful."

Devine was ready forty minutes later. In my car, I followed him to a bar on the edge of the ghetto—The Easy Dollar. I gave him a minute, and followed him in. I slipped into a booth in the deepest shadow. I was nervous, and glad Devine was there. We all want the police around when they're doing their job.

A bulky man sat on the bar stool next to Devine. They didn't talk to each other, or didn't seem to. Then Devine walked away. As he opened the door, light fell on the man who had been next to him.

It was the massive bullet-head who had taught me a boxing lesson in The Carleton Club parking lot.

31 ⌒

PERRY LINT HAD MONEY, and he was thirsty. I was alone in his territory, and he knew my face. Every drink he ordered, my stomach went down a notch. I hoped Devine hadn't gone too far, the bartender would wonder why I didn't order another drink soon. I didn't dare; drinkers have a way of looking around when another man orders.

He had five. I lost a pound with each one. But after the fifth he looked at his watch, paid, and stood up. Going out, he filled the whole doorway—a walking redwood stump. I had to risk staying fairly close. I hoped he didn't walk into the ghetto. There I'd stand out like a neon sign. I was lucky.

Outside, he ambled like a bear to a faded-red Ford sedan, invulnerable, so looking only straight ahead. I sprinted for my car. He drove slow and erratically—drunk and knew it. I settled down closer than normal, and hoped he was drunk enough. He turned away from the ghetto, and cruised easily on through the city. Soon we were on the county highway in the direction of the old mining town suburb of Nugget.

I was getting a feel of excitement. Perry Lint had looked at his watch after his fifth drink. He hadn't wanted to leave the bar, but he had. It looked like he had an appointment. I hoped he did. If he didn't, I was going to have to try to talk to him, and he wasn't going to want to talk.

A mile this side of Nugget, he pulled into a side road, and stopped about sixty feet in before a big, old frame house in a state of medium neglect. A Cadillac stood in the drive of the old house. It looked familiar. Perry Lint parked behind the Cadillac, climbed out, and walked up the porch steps. I was parked on the shoulder of the highway near a fruit stand, but Lint never looked around anyway. I guessed that he wasn't much of a detective. He did other work.

I drove on, U-turned, and came back to park in front of a fenced house just before the side road. I worked my way to the big house. There was no cover for the last twenty feet. I squatted, hidden, where I could see the front door. It was a long wait.

At three-ten the door opened and Perry Lint came out. He wasn't alone. I knew why the Cadillac had been familiar. I saw the pink face, arrogant mouth, and big frame of Scott Keating. He was a long way from Pasadena, or Max Alfreda's theater. He didn't shake hands with Perry Lint. The black man took no notice. Lint lived in a hustler's world with little bigotry—every man was an enemy.

I waited until Lint drove off in his red Ford. I could find Lint any time. I waited until I was sure he was far away. Then I walked to the porch and the front door. Keating himself answered the door—and tried to close it.

I kicked it open. He wasn't old, and he kept fit every easy day, but he was soft inside. He wouldn't take even a bruise for any cause. He backed away to a shaded living room from the time when everyone in California who wasn't Spanish built homes just like those they'd left in Boston. The room was furnished with polished old pieces that glowed like velvet.

I said, "Now I want real answers, Keating."

"I have influence here, you get out!" he sputtered.

His face was flushed. Part of it was outrage, but there was fear too. Physical fear, his eyes on my fists, and some other fear. His pale eyes hopped around as if they didn't belong to him, the boy looking out again through his middle-aged face.

"I want Judy Carlos, Keating."

"I don't know a Judy Carlos."

"Max Alfreda does, and you work with Alfreda!"

"He doesn't know anything, either! After our talk, I asked him. He knows nothing about your Judy Carlos."

"You asked him? When? Where?"

"Here, a few days ago." He chewed his lip.

"Where's Alfreda now?"

"He returned to Los Angeles, of course."

"No, he didn't," I said. I would have heard. I tried an old trick. "Pete Wallace says you know Judy Carlos well."

I lost the gamble. He stiffened. Every man has some bone in him somewhere. He seemed suddenly to have found solid ground, some confidence.

He shook his head. "No, you're wrong. I never met any Judy Carlos."

"But you know Frank Carlos."

"I know of him, yes."

"What are you doing up here? It's not Pasadena."

"I have property here. San Perdido is my family home. This was our house for many generations. We're an old family, Shaw. My father still lives here. We helped to build this country. My wife, however, prefers Pasadena and Los Angeles."

"What does Perry Lint prefer, Keating? Besides beating people in parking lots?"

He stepped back, his hands up before his face as if he expected me to hit him. I only watched him. When he realized that I wasn't going to hit, he tried a contrite smile.

"I . . . I'm sorry about that. A mistake," he said. "Perry Lint was waiting for me in L.A., so when I left Alfreda's that evening I told him to beat you up to discourage you from digging around into my affairs. I was afraid you'd find out . . ."

He stopped, so I finished it for him. "Afraid I'd find out about you spying on the Panthers, tipping the police? Just what's your interest in the Panthers, Keating?"

He studied my face as if trying to find out what I knew, detect a trick. Then his mouth tightened. He nodded to some voice in his head, suddenly confident. Had I found his cause?

"My interest is the country, Shaw," he said, his voice firm. "The Panthers are dangerous, you know that as well as I do. A group of us here decided to take positive action. We hired Perry Lint to help us destroy the Panthers by tipping the police when to raid them."

"Vigilante technique again? Like the old days?"

"What else are the Panthers, Shaw, but vigilantes?"

I had to give him the point. So much in life depends on where you stand, what you believe—with or without good reason.

"All for the country, Keating?" I said. "Or does your group maybe have more tangible motives? Like property, and power, and control of the country?"

His mouth went thinner. "We all have property here, yes. Is it wrong to protect one's property? Our country is built on property, Shaw. In the strike I lost a $300,000 building."

"Does that make Frank Carlos a target for you, too?"

"He's even worse than the others. He was a state employee. He should have been shot dead!"

"Did you try to do that, Keating? As well as beat me up?"

"No! I don't kill!"

"Someone tried to kill Carlos. You sent Lint to get me."

"I sent Lint to discourage you looking, no more. I sent no one to kill Carlos, or anyone else!"

I believed him. I had escaped because I had been in the open, and because Lint and his partner had not been trying to kill me. Frank Carlos had been alone in an isolated house, and his attackers had intended to kill. Perry Lint would not have been stopped by a gun in the hand of a badly wounded man.

"Why do you really pay Alfreda money, Keating? You're no theater-lover, and you're not his backer."

He bit at his petulant lip. "With his violent ideas, he's involved with subversives. He is in direct contact with the Panthers. I decided he could be used. He's so neutral about disorder that he actually helps us. Objective about violence!"

"Do you know a Rick Elliot?"

"No."

"And you used Perry Lint to tip the police when it was good to raid the Panthers?"

He nodded, proudly. "I'll deny it, of course. No proof."

"Except Perry Lint."

It didn't seem to worry him. He didn't think Perry Lint would talk. Neither did I. At least, not easily.

"Where does Lint get his information?" I asked. "He's not a Panther. He's well known, they wouldn't trust him."

"He never tells us that."

I believed that, too. "A woman?"

"I don't know, Shaw."

In the dim and slimy world of hustlers, a man protects his sources. He'd better, if he wants to eat and stay alive.

"I'd be careful with Lint," I said.

"No, we have what he wants—money. He's no danger."

"Too bad you can't buy the Panthers."

"We'll destroy them instead, Shaw."

"Unless they stop you."

"We have the weapons, and the power."

I didn't like it, but it was the truth. At least for now. I left him with his power in that living room that was a relic of a better past. No, not better, only that the hate and violence of that era had not been opposed by its silent victims.

I walked down the road to my car this time. My eyes were alert for any sign of the red Ford and Perry Lint. I didn't see the Ford, but I saw the black sedan. It looked like the same sedan I'd seen outside Keating's house in Pasadena. There were four people in it again, and it was parked off the highway near the same fruit stand where I had watched Perry Lint stop at Keating's house.

When I reached the highway, I started across toward the car. The sun glinted on the windows, and I couldn't see inside. The car pulled away. Traffic blocked me. I ran at an angle to try to see inside the car, but it screamed its tires, and was gone among the other speeding cars.

I walked to my car. I found a telephone booth and called Lieutenant Devine. He had no news. John Morgan and his wife were still missing, but if Scott Keating was telling the truth, Judy might not be part of any public violence at all.

Which made Max Alfreda, and Emil Tarra and his mountain cabin, a lot more important.

32

I STOPPED on the road for dinner, and Max Alfreda's theater was silent in the night when I got there. Our stake-out had nothing to report. I drove to our office. Delaney was at his desk.

"Your wife is a caged tiger. Take her to Mexico, okay?"

"What's a partner for," I said. "Keep her happy."

"Who keeps Thayer happy about costs? Can Carlos pay?"

"Take it out of my share. What about Carlos?"

"The guard's off. You want my guess? The sheriff's going to file it unsolved and forget it. Maybe we should."

I turned for the door.

Delaney swore behind me. "Damn it, okay! You want to hear what else I have?"

I turned back. "What?"

"I did some work on Rick Elliot. His drive on that Wednesday was up toward San Perdido, a garage man told me. I dug into his past, and it seems he was away a lot even before he ran into your girl. Sometimes for days. The wife, Joanne, goes to Palm Springs a lot, but there were times she vanished from the Springs just when Ricky-boy was away from home."

"Checking on him?"

"Who knows? Last, but not least, Elliot slipped our stake-out this afternoon, and took off. Sorry, Paul."

"Anyone can slip a stake-out if they spot it," I said. "Tell Maureen I'll call her later."

I went back down to my car. There was a lot of traffic on Wilshire, and more people walking than usual. It took me ten minutes to reach The Carleton Club. The attendant charged up and grabbed my car, and I marched in once more. The bodyguard, Lou, met me, and we did the parade through the curtain. With a difference. The weapons-detector rang the alarm.

"Hold it!" Lou said. He had a hand in his pocket.

"I forgot," I said. I pulled my Colt out by the butt, handed it to him.

He pocketed it, then knocked on Emil Tarra's door. It buzzed me inside. It was later this time, and Tarra had a drink. He offered me one with a wave. I shook my head.

He shrugged. "You doing any better than the cops?"

"I think so."

"That lover-boy mixed in?"

"Maybe," I said. "It depends who Judy was planning to go to the cabin with."

He drank, savored the whiskey. "Cabin?"

"That's right. You didn't mention the cabin, did you? Maybe you forgot."

He put his glass down like a western gunman moving an object out of his way to have a clear field of fire in some saloon shoot-out. He looked up at me.

"I told you at the start, Shaw, I like Judy, what she does is her business. She asked to use my cabin, I said she could, it had nothing to do with her being missing. Just the opposite, I'd figure. If she wasn't missing, she might have used it."

"Why? How the hell do you know that?"

"Because she's missing from the husband, right?"

"Yes, but—"

He sat back. "She wanted the cabin to take some time away from the rat race with him. With her husband."

"With Frank Carlos? You're sure?"

"Damn it, I don't say things I'm not sure of," Tarra snapped. "She said she wanted to use the cabin for a week or so when she could arrange it for them to go."

"Where is the cabin?"

"In the mountains, near Nugget."

"Didn't you think how close to San Perdido that is? You knew she went to San Perdido. She could have gone to the cabin with someone else."

"I've got better things to think about."

"She had the keys?"

"Wouldn't need them. I keep some there, told her where."

"Have you been up there since?"

"No."

"A caretaker?"

"No. It's just a small place for being alone."

"Then you don't know if she's been there or not."

"Look, Shaw," Tarra said, "she's a girl who works in my club. I like her, but I don't go around—"

His telephone rang. He swore, "Damn," and picked it up.

He listened, handed the receiver to me. "For you."

I took it. "Shaw speaking, what—?"

The soft chuckle chilled my spine. "Hello, darling."

33 ⌒

MY MIND ECHOED her voice, heard the past: *"Paul? Darling? I miss you. Oh, I miss you."*

I said, "Judy? Where the hell—?"

"Paul? Darling? I'm in trouble, real trouble. I didn't know you were looking for me until today."

Her voice, six years, but it rang and echoed: *"Paul? I'm married. Tonight. I just got married today . . . Paul? I'm in trouble . . ."*

I said, "Where've you been, Judy?"

Her soft voice shook, but I could see her trying to smile, wherever she was. "Hiding, Paul. In a cabin. They want to kill me. I'm so scared, darling. Weeks I've been there. I had to try, come out, and I heard about you. So—"

"Who wants to kill you, Judy?"

"I don't know, not for sure. Max Alfreda is part of it, I know that. Maybe . . . Frank . . . I . . . I can't talk from here any more. Paul, I need you."

"Paul? I miss you, darling. Oh, I miss you." I shook my head to clear the fog of past and present mixing in my ears.

"Who else? Judy? Why do they—?"

Fear in her whisper. "I have to go! Paul? I'll try to come to your office. Later. Please, Paul?"

"Judy?"

The line was dead. Not cut off, no. She had hung up. Where? My office. Then she had to be somewhere in Los Angeles. Tarra was watching me.

"She's in trouble? She sounded scared. Her voice," he said.

"They're trying to kill her," I said. My mind wouldn't function right. My brain was numb, filled with the echoes of the past, our past. *I'm Judy Tower . . . no lies, Paul . . .*"

"Who's trying to kill her?" Tarra said.

"She doesn't know. Max Alfreda. Maybe Frank Carlos. All she could say—"

I turned and walked out of there. My office. I walked fast. Lou, the bodyguard, had to stop me to give me my gun. I don't know what I tipped the attendant.

The office was empty when I got there. Delaney was gone. I looked everywhere. Then I sat down. I put my gun on my desk. I waited.

34 🪶

WAS IT A TRICK?

Had it been Judy? Her voice? *"Paul? Darling? I miss you. Oh, I miss you."* Yes! Low, a whisper and afraid, but her voice, of course it was.

But—not exactly her voice. Six years. That long since I had heard her voice. How could I really be sure? It could be a trick, a trap. Except that she had not asked me to meet her anywhere, no. She would come here, to the office—and how could that be a trap?

No, she *sounded* like Judy. Her pattern of words, the way she called me "darling." Too much risk for a stranger trying to trick me to use any endearment. It could so easily have been the wrong one.

What she had told me fit what I knew. I had found no trace of her after the call to Rick Elliot that Tuesday almost three weeks ago. It fit with being in hiding in a cabin, and I knew there was a cabin. Max Alfreda had vanished from his theater—the most important thing in his life. It fitted.

Frank Carlos suddenly anxious to find her after two weeks. Because, maybe, he had failed to find her, and hoped that I could smoke her out because she trusted me? That could fit.

Then who had tried to kill Carlos, and who, besides Keating, had tried to stop me, and killed Gloria Kazko? A falling-out of conspirators? It happens. A third force? Maybe Keating told only part of the truth?

I looked again at the clock: 2:00 A.M.

I fought sleep. I lost.

I jerked awake: 3:17 A.M.

I got up and walked, never far from the pistol.

Where was she? Lost again? So close to her, and maybe to all the answers? To hell with the answers. She was alive! Or was she by now? So near, and then too late?

The clock inched past 4:00 A.M.

I went to the front windows and looked out. The side street was deserted. A lone man came from Wilshire Boulevard, walking slowly, and passed under our windows and out of sight up the street. On Wilshire there was traffic, growing heavier with the approach of dawn. I . . .

The telephone rang. I had it. "Judy?"

"I couldn't be sure, Paul." Her voice tight and shaky. "They're somewhere close, I feel it. I had to try—"

"Come to the office, fast."

The edge of panic in her voice, "No! The lobby, it's too open, too light." But the intense life still there, too. Not easily defeated. "I'm getting away, Paul. Out of the country. No other way now, darling."

"Judy, listen—"

"Maybe France, you know? They have fine theater there," she said, and I could see in my mind that distant look in her big eyes. "But . . . I want to see you, darling. Once more."

"Where are you? I've got a gun."

"On Wilshire. In a telephone booth. A damned goldfish." I imagined her looking out at the dark night from inside the lighted glass cubicle. "I . . . There's a real estate office near. I can see it. I—"

"I know where it is."

"I'll wait there, in the doorway. Hurry . . ."

I hung up. I picked up my gun, put it into my pocket, my hand on it. I walked fast down the stairs. I turned left. I walked fast toward Wilshire.

All the time my mind had only one thought—now it could be the trap. Now she had asked me to come out of my office into a dark night street—to meet her at a definite place.

At the corner of Wilshire, three early-rising men hurried along ahead of me. The real estate office was across the wide street, half a block from the corner of my street. It had a deeply recessed entrance between storefront windows lettered in gold. I let the three men walk ahead of me, blending close behind them, scanning the opposite side of Wilshire from my side, where I had a wider view.

When I came abreast of the real estate office, I looked toward the shadowed doorway across the night street. I didn't stop walking yet, close behind the three men.

She emerged from the shadows of the recessed doorway. I saw her in the light of a streetlamp, small and dark-haired, in a green minidress that clung to her round body under an open raincoat. She saw me, smiled, and waved. That eager wave, urging me to hurry across the boulevard, as she looked up and down the dark street.

Two cars hurried past, blocking me, and then a third car came. From my right—slowly. Too slowly, and then suddenly speeding up and moving closer to the far sidewalk where Judy stood. I began to run, my gun out.

"Judy!" I shouted.

She ran to the left, the raincoat streaming out. The car, a small black Ford, gunned its motor as it went after her. I went down on one knee in the middle of the street, and fired at its tires. It roared away along Wilshire. I was up and running. I couldn't see Judy. I ran left the way she had run, and came to the first cross street. The black Ford was gone.

Down the cross street, almost at the next corner, I saw her still running in panic, the raincoat streaming.

"Judy! It's all right! Judy!"

She reached a small car. She didn't hear me at the distance, or she didn't care now, running for the safety she knew. She was inside the small car. It started, and pulled careening away, its tires burning on the concrete.

A yellow sports car. Like the yellow sports car I had seen that first day on the road to Frank Carlos' Malibu house.

I ran another block, shouting, trying to catch the yellow car, but it was out of sight now.

I walked back to Wilshire.

I walked across Wilshire, around the corner, and up to my office. I put my pistol on the desk, sat down, and let my breathing slow. I lighted a cigarette, and looked at the telephone. Would she call again? Yes. She had to call again. Or did she? Leaving the country, and she had a car.

Had the man in the yellow sports car been trying to reach Frank Carlos for her that first day? Or had he been watching Carlos for her? A friend looking for her? Or did the car belong to those who were after her, and somehow she had stolen it?

I watched the telephone the way a child watches a toy just out of its reach.

I fell asleep.

The footsteps woke me. In the corridor. My clock read 9:12 A.M. I picked up my pistol. The footsteps stopped outside.

The outer door opened, the feet hurried across the outer office, and my door opened.

I held the gun in both hands, aimed at his chest.

He stopped. Small and brown, his hair a great halo, his eyes hidden by the dark glasses. Pete Wallace.

He said, "She was at our headquarters on that Tuesday night. Judy. I came down fast to tell you."

35 ～

I LOWERED THE GUN. "How'd you find out?"

He sat down. "There's a creep up in the ghetto. Stoolie, hustler, muscleman, you name it. Everything dirty, he does."

"Perry Lint?"

"You know him?" Pete seemed surprised.

"I know him," I said. "What about him?"

"He got word I was looking around for Judy, and came to me. He knew her from the strike days. For a taste of the beard, he told me he'd seen her goin' into our headquarters around seven-thirty that night."

It had the sound of Perry Lint—play all angles for a dollar. If someone would pay for something he knew, he'd sell it no matter what else it might do, or whom it might compromise.

"Can you trust him?" I said.

"Hell no. But when he told me, I went to work on one of the brothers owes me favors, and who don't trust Johnny Morgan too far, neither. He admitted Judy was there! She talked with Morgan and Felicia. She left about nine P.M., and Johnny Morgan went out right after." His eyes seemed to glitter behind the dark glasses. "Now Morgan and Felicia're both missing, Paul. While I was still in jail, the cops busted our headquarters again. Morgan and Felicia wasn't there, no one's seen 'em since."

"I know," I said. "I've seen Judy, Pete. She called last night. Someone's trying to kill her."

"You saw her? Hell, that's great!" He went from smile to frown in a second as my last words sank in. "Kill her? Who?"

"She doesn't know. Have you seen Max Alfreda?"

He shook his head. "Not since that day you did."

"He's been away from his theater since last Tuesday night."

"Mr. Max? That's crazy! Mr. Max'd never stay away from his theater so long."

"That's what I think," I said, and I told him everything that had happened last night. "It looks like Alfreda is mixed in it, and maybe Carlos. I think I better talk to Frank."

He was up. "Yeh, can I go along? Jesus, if Judy's alive, and someone's after her, I—"

"Let's go, then," I said.

I got my car, and Pete followed me in his old Chevy wagon. There was a slow-down on the Freeway, and I swore the whole way to the hospital where they still had Frank Carlos. We went in the front way this time. As Delaney had told me, the guard was off, and Frank Carlos was sitting up in a chair when we came in. He was doing nothing. He didn't seem anxious to leave.

"You took your time," he said to me.

"I got busy," I said. "You know Pete Wallace?"

"Sure," Pete said, smiling at Carlos.

"We've met," Frank Carlos said. But it wasn't Pete he was interested in. "You find out anything, Shaw?"

"Some," I said, and said, "I talked to Judy last night, Frank. I saw her."

He came out of that chair on a string, and grabbed at his side, gasping. "She's all right? You have her? Where?"

I shook my head. "She ran, Frank. She was scared off."

"You—?" He was bent over, holding his side. Slowly he straightened up, breathed easier. "You lost her again?"

I told him all that had happened. "She saw me across Wilshire. She waved at me, smiled. Then this damned car roared up. It scared her, and she ran. I lost her."

He was seeing her in his mind. "Green dress, yes? It was raining that Monday. She took her raincoat. I'd forgotten. She had her raincoat the last time I saw—"

It was what I'd needed to be sure. I said, "She told me someone was trying to kill her, Frank. She didn't know who, but she mentioned you!"

"Me? That's crazy! Why would she say I wanted to kill her? You're lying!" His dark eyes blazed at me, the faint Oriental cast making them like the eyes of a tiger.

"No," I said. "She was scared, confused. Maybe she saw or heard something that gave her the idea. Or maybe somebody told her something against you."

"What could anyone tell her?" His voice was very cold.

"You tell me that, Frank," I said.

"Nothing! And Judy wouldn't believe anything, anyway. She'd never get that idea no matter how scared! You're lying, both of you. Why? What's Wallace got to do with this?"

"We're not lying, Carlos," I said. "Pete just likes Judy, too. He worked with her, right?"

"That stinking ghetto theater of his?" Frank Carlos said, and laughed nastily. "She hated that theater, I told you. No talent, no taste, a washout! Tell me why you're lying?"

"If anyone's lying, Carlos, it's Judy. Why would she lie?"

He stood there—very tall, and very silent now. I sensed he was hardly seeing us at all. Working something out in his mind, groping for his thoughts. Perhaps trying to put Judy, and what she had said, together with the attempt to kill him. He was still standing that way, while Pete Wallace and I watched him, when a nurse came in.

"You two wait outside a minute, I have to examine Mr. Carlos."

Frank Carlos' eyes moved to look at the nurse. Pete Wallace and I went out into the corridor. Pete stood against a wall, both hands in the pockets of his leather jacket, that sneer he used for the whole white world back on his face as he watched nurses and doctors pass. An orderly approached us.

"One of you Paul Shaw?"

"I am," I said.

"Telephone. You can take it at the nurses' station."

Pete hurried with me to the telephone. Who knew I was here? Dick Delaney was the only possibility—something about Max Alfreda, maybe? Or Maureen. I grabbed the receiver.

"Paul Shaw," I said.

The hospital switchboard girl said, "Just a moment, please."

I waited.

I waited too long. The line was silent. Pete Wallace watched me, his face questioning. I shook my head. I said, "Hello? Hello? Who is it? Hello?" But there was only the silence, and . . . I slammed down the receiver.

"Pete, damn it! Come on!"

I ran back down the corridor. We both burst into Frank Carlos' room at the same time, and stopped. The room was empty. Pete whirled, ran back out into the corridor. I went to the single closet. It was empty. No clothes. Pete came back.

"Nowhere, man! He's gone!"

"Yes," I said, "and in his clothes. The call was a neat trick to get us away. The question is—where has he gone?"

"To Judy, Paul? He knows where to find her?"

"I don't know," I said. "I think he was really surprised when I told him I'd seen her, talked to her. Only why was he surprised? Because I'd found her alive, or because I'd seen her when he thought she was held safely somewhere? Surprised to find her alive, or surprised to find her on the loose?"

"Yeh, man, that's a difference, you know?" Pete said.

I thought—hard. Everyone was on the move, and I couldn't be everywhere at once. Judy wouldn't try to contact me again, I realized. No. She would be afraid that they, whoever they, or him, happened to be, knew now that she wanted to get to me, and would watch me. Either I charged around after all the missing suspects, or I tried to pick up her trail.

"Pete, you want to try to find John Morgan and his wife? Go back to San Perdido and see if you can? Maybe keep an eye open for Carlos too?"

"Okay, Paul, I'll like that anyway. I want to know what the hell Morgan's pulling," he said. "How about you?"

"I'm going to try to find Judy again," I said. I didn't add, before it's too late for good this time—but I thought it.

Pete drove off in his old wagon, and I called Delaney and Maureen. Delaney had nothing to report. Maureen was getting edgy, she wanted to get out of the hospital, and she wanted me with her. Judy was taking up a lot of my time. I could hear the doubt growing in her voice. They were doubts I couldn't answer.

The doubts were still in my mind as I drove north. I had seen Judy again. The hard lump down in my guts was something I didn't want to think about.

Hunger and fatigue caught up with me two thirds of the way to Nugget and Emil Tarra's mountain cabin. It was the only place I could hope to pick up Judy's trail, and I needed to be in the best shape possible when I got there.

I pulled off the Freeway to eat a brunch and sleep a few hours. I slept three hours. Then I started on again—through Nugget, and up into the first slopes of the towering Sierras.

36 ☞

IN THE NEAREST VILLAGE, they directed me to a side gravel road that wound among the long slopes of forested mountains. Snow was deep on the ground, the pungent smell of wood smoke heavy in the cold air of the afternoon. The snow of the road was deeply rutted by the frequent passage of cars. I passed two large lodges set snugly on boulders overlooking the sweeping Sierra valley. After that, there was nothing for a mile.

Emil Tarra's cabin was small, and built on a point of land that jutted out into a pond at the bottom of the valley. Cars had been here, the snow rutted, but not many cars. The only neighbor was a cluster of three large, low, rambling buildings built of unpainted boards, with few windows, and all marked with large wooden crosses. The cross-marked buildings were a good quarter of a mile away along the road, and higher, looking down on the cabin. I parked, tried the door. It was open.

I went into a simple, rustic cabin—a place to be alone, as Tarra had said. I couldn't see Emil Tarra coming here, but you can never know all about anyone. There is that slimy underbelly of the pure, and the simple underside of the tough and complex. I checked the cabin, gun in hand, but no one was there.

I searched. There was little to search. I found food, mostly canned, but not much. No garbage container. Here, garbage would be buried. Everything was neat—as if someone had tried to keep busy. The double bed had been slept in, unmade and rumpled. There was no booze. In a corner I found a woman's lipstick—a brunette shade. I also found some blood.

Not a lot of blood, but some, not far from the bed. I looked at it for a time. It was perhaps two weeks old, but could have been older or fresher. More blood than from some small cut, but a long way from being a lot of blood.

I found the newspaper behind the bed—the San Perdido paper for Tuesday, February 3. The last day anyone admitted seeing Judy—and the day she said she had come up here.

After that, I turned the place upside down looking for any lead to where she might have gone. I found nothing.

I went outside and searched the snow. I had no coat, and I shivered in the mountain-afternoon cold. But I found nothing. I studied the tire tracks. They told me only that more than one car had been here within the last month or so. Some tracks had been snowed on in the open, showed up only under the carport. One set of tracks looked like those of a sports car.

Freezing, I went back inside and took a heavy jacket out of the closet where I had seen it. It was too small—Emil Tarra's jacket—but it was warm. Outside again, I walked up the road to the cluster of unpainted buildings marked with crosses. As I walked, I studied the road and the bordering woods. At the first of the three cross-marked buildings a handsome young man with a small beard answered my knock. He wore a brown, hooded robe exactly like the one worn by Max Alfreda. But this man had it belted with a chain and rosary.

"Yes, friend?" he said pleasantly.

I told him who I was. "I'd like to ask some questions about that cabin down there."

"Mr. Tarra's cabin? Come in."

I went in. The building was one large room—a communal dining hall, recreation room, workshop all combined. Some sixteen men sat around, reading or working on some craft work. They all wore the same brown robe, and most were bearded. My guide smiled.

"We're a small, religious family, Mr. Shaw. We were not pleased with our larger order. When our superiors would not listen to us, we decided to band together on our own, come out here into the wilderness to find our own life and way to God."

"You built this all yourselves?"

He laughed. "Every board and nail, with many bloody thumbs, I can tell you. All city boys, to a man. Now we are self-sufficient. We write our own hymns, kill our own meat. Live with nature every day, and so worship God."

An older monk came to us. "We did not leave our church, we found ourselves within it. We had become religious robots. Now we know that shelter is not built of money, and meat does not come in plastic boxes. We understand the design."

A muscular one said, "Will our guest join us for dinner?"

"Yes," the first one agreed.

I said, "I'm sorry, but thank you. You look like you work hard for what you have."

"We do," the older one said, "but for us the work and

what we work for are the same. You are a friend of Mr. Tarra?"

"In a way," I said. "Has he been to the cabin recently?"

"No," the first one said, "but others have been. Earlier today, a few hours ago, another man was there."

"What did he look like?"

"At this distance? A tall man, no more. In a gray VW."

Another monk said, "Last night a car came, quite late. A black car, I believe, with more than one person."

"Some weeks ago there were people," the first one said. "They made noise, but it was night. They did not stay long."

"Have you seen anyone living there. Say, for two weeks?"

"No. There have been no lights, no one we saw."

I thanked them, and walked back to the cabin and my car. The afternoon was fading fast in the mountains, growing colder. The man today before me had to be Frank Carlos. Had I told him about the cabin? Yes, I had—if Carlos had needed me to tell him.

The car last night, had it been a black car? John Morgan, maybe, who was missing? Or David Eigen, who had been in love with Judy?

There was always Scott Keating, who hired muscle to serve his cause, and maybe Judy had gotten in his way.

Two weeks ago "some people" had come to the cabin. Maybe Judy's enemies looking for her, chasing her down? They had not stayed long, so maybe she had evaded them, and then hidden here as a safe place once they had looked and not found her. The monks had seen no one, and no light, but she would have stayed hidden and kept the windows covered. Some woman had been in the cabin—a brunette woman. And the newspaper was from San Perdido for the day Judy had vanished.

I drove out of the mountain valley.

37 🐾

PETE WALLACE'S HOUSE at the edge of the quarry in San Perdido was dark and silent. No one answered my knocking.

I drove on along Fremont Street to David Eigen's place. I went up to his apartment, and found a girl sitting alone. She was reading. I asked her where Eigen was.

"Is it important?" the girl said. "Dave's had a bad time. He was arrested for nothing, and sat in jail for three days!"

"So did I," I said, "and it's important."

"You were in that prison?" There was admiration in her young eyes. I was a hero of the fight against the Establishment. She wished she had been in that prison. The event was going to become a legend of the fight.

"With a lot of others," I said. "Where is Eigen?"

"He's relaxing, he needs rest. He went over to The Circle to meditate."

"Where is it?"

"South Diego Street. Number 97. It's not far," and she told me how to find South Diego Street.

I drove through the night city, and located South Diego Street a block from The Easy Dollar bar, where I'd picked up Perry Lint. The streets were empty, and I parked near The Easy Dollar where the ghetto began, and walked. South Diego was a dark, narrow street that faded on into the ghetto. Number 97 was on the first block.

The building was pitch-dark. My hopes went down to zero. There had been so little to get my teeth into. I'd found Judy, and lost her. I was beginning to feel how the real police felt every day of their lives—walking around in jelly, hoping someone would call and tell them who did what to whom.

I stared at that building. Only two stories high, like a small warehouse. It stood all alone, apart from the other buildings, and looked—condemned? I walked closer. It was condemned! The first-floor windows were all boarded up, and signs were nailed onto the front boards. Old signs.

I crossed the street, and began to circle the building. At the rear second-story windows I saw a very faint hint of light, as if they were covered inside. I circled all the way to the rear, and saw a black doorway, and faint stairs inside.

A yellow sports car was parked close to the condemned building in the rear shadows.

I got out my pistol, approached the car. It was empty. There was no registration inside anywhere.

I went inside the dark entrance and took the stairs up, fast and quiet. A thin line of light came from under the door at the top. I didn't knock. My pistol ready, I kicked the door in. It was old and rotten and it went in one kick. I jumped inside, my gun held in front of me.

The room was large—the width of the condemned building, and half the length, with a plywood partition shutting off the front half of the building. Blankets hung over the windows. The only furniture was a few boxes, a large Primus cookstove, two oil heaters, and mattresses scattered all across the bare wood floor. All the stoves were going, the air hot and stifling and smelling of oil.

Seven faces looked at me.

A young girl, at least five months pregnant, stood at the stove, stirring something in a large pot. Bread, milk, and Cokes were on a box beside her, chipped plates stacked ready.

Two more girls lay together on a double mattress. They were propped on their elbows reading. One had an open notebook beside her, the other smoked a thin brown cigarette, taking slow, deep puffs as I watched.

A woman in her late twenties sat against a wall, all alone. She wore a long purple sack dress that shone in the candle-light. Her face was made up in bizarre colors and black lines. Her breasts hung heavy and loose under the purple, and her eyes were vague, dilated.

A young man with shaggy hair and a thick mustache lay on a mattress with another young girl. He wore only a shirt. The girl kissed him lightly, softly, and they both watched me.

David Eigen lay on a mattress, alone, looking up at the ceiling, smoking another thin brown cigarette.

None of them moved as I stood there half crouched, my gun out in front of me. They only turned their heads to look, all except the older girl with the vague, dilated eyes. She looked at nothing, her painted face like a savage mask.

Silent, watching, waiting—like small animals watching a tiger break into their lair. Immobile in the thick, hot air of the room, without panic or reaction, as if they were too aware of danger and pain to react when threatened. What would happen, would happen; and movement would not save them. All chance and fate, so they sat without re-sponse—but not without teeth. I saw in their cold, flat eyes the small razor-sharp teeth they could use on me if they had the chance. But I held the bigger weapon, so they only watched.

The man in the shirt said, "Is this a bust, Mr. Fuzz? You have some kind of warrant?"

His voice was quiet, educated. He didn't seem scared, and the girl beside him went on kissing him lightly.

"I'm not the police," I said.

David Eigen lay back on his mattress. "He's a private eye, looking for Judy Carlos. He loves Judy, too."

"Judy flies," one of the reading girls said, looking at me with more interest. "She's heard her voices. Lucky."

"Is she here?" I asked.

David Eigen said, "She's where she wants to be, Judy. No doubts, no time for trivia like me."

"She's not here," the reading girl said.

The girl at the stove arched her pregnant back. "Are you hungry, private eye? It's a good stew."

"No, thanks," I said. I squatted down beside David Eigen, holstered my gun. "What is this place, Eigen?"

His dark eyes were high, but not high enough to hide the despair in their depths. A despair that was no part of his public life, and so much a part of his inner life. A strong mind in a fearful body. Afraid of pain and women, facing up to both as best he could. A braver man than most, because his courage wasn't natural, an act of will.

"The Circle," he said. "Call it a co-operative haven, a place to be alone away from *them*." He shivered. "They beat me more in that prison. Students and police, we have to be enemies, don't we? The job of the cops to enforce the law as it is. The job of students to study and question the laws. Cops have to feel the law is always right, can't change. Students have to feel all law is imperfect, must change. Yes. No way."

I said, "I saw Judy last night. Someone is trying to kill her. Why? Who?"

The fear danced in his eyes. "You saw her? That's good."

"You didn't think I'd find her alive?"

"No. Judy . . . doesn't hide out."

"Because she's a spy against the Panthers, or some other reason? A private reason?"

"Someone tried to kill Frank Carlos, didn't they?"

"Do you know why?"

"You can't quit," he said. "You're part of history, even on the fringe."

I said, "There's a yellow sports car outside, Eigen. Who owns it?"

"Yellow sports car?" His eyes jumped around again.

"If Judy isn't here, who drove that car here?"

"Not here, Mr. Shaw. I—"

I stopped him. "No, Eigen. That car's parked behind this building. There's nowhere else for the driver to be. Are you driving it, Eigen? That—"

I heard movement, turned fast. The woman in her late twenties, with the painted face and vague eyes, was up and on her way toward the plywood partition. I saw the hand-cut door in the partition for the first time.

"Not me," David Eigen said. "No one here drives a yellow sports car. Maybe somebody was just parking it there for a time."

I watched the woman go through the door. Eigen continued to talk behind me, and I heard the tension in his voice. A tension I heard better because I was not looking at him.

He was babbling now, nervous and taut: "Around here people just park and go away. Sometimes for days. No hurry, everyone does what he—"

I was already up and walking toward the partition when I heard the noise. Movement on the other side of the thin wall. I ran to the open door and through it, grabbing my gun out again. Someone jumped on me.

Silk and fingernails, a snarling painted face in the very dim light, and loose, heavy breasts against me. Through her clawing, as I beat her off, I saw a man and a girl running the other way toward the front of the building.

I slapped the clawing painted woman hard. She went down in a flurry of curses. I aimed the pistol at the two backs running ahead.

"Hold it! Stop!"

They didn't stop. Either they ran in total panic, or they knew I wasn't going to shoot. Talk and answers was what I had to have, and maybe they knew that. They ran out of sight.

I chased.

There was a door at the front, a flight of shaky stairs

going down. I plunged on down, skidding flat on a loose board, and coming down hard at the bottom. I swore and struggled up. The side outer door was open, swinging. I ran on out into the darkness. I saw them back at the rear of the building, going around the corner toward where the yellow car was. A shaft of random light showed the dark hair of the girl, her streaming raincoat. She was being pulled by the hand by the long-haired man as they went around the corner.

"Judy!" I shouted.

I reached the corner. They were at the yellow car. I had them! They stopped trying to get into the car. The man turned to face me. I walked with my gun out.

The shadow moved behind and to my right. I didn't have time to turn.

My head took the blow—something hard and soft, a blackjack.

On my knees, trying to get up.

Hit again . . . and again . . .

38 ⌒

I WAS ON MY KNEES, hands flat on the ground. My head hung down. I heard cars moving, the sound of horns, the squeal of tires. But far off, not near. Distant voices.

I sat down in the dirt. I felt my head. Where I'd been hit, it was sticky. But not too bad. Tapped, not slammed or killed. Why? Too close to home? Too easy for the police to know who had killed me? Or just a mistake—hit and run.

Someone there in the shadows of the building. Anyone.

One of those upstairs who had come down the shorter way. Eigen?

I looked at my watch. Five minutes, less. I tested the rest of me. All present and working. My gun was in its holster. Nice of them. I searched my pockets. Keys still there, but nothing else. Stripped clean of money, wallet, papers. Why leave me my gun?

I smelled the whiskey.

I stood up, swayed, and looked at myself. My shirt was stained and wet, my tie gone. My suit jacket was grimy and smelled of whiskey. The left pocket of my jacket bulged. It was full of something like loose tobacco. I dumped it out, smelled it: *pot, tea, gage*—marijuana.

I knew why I had been left my gun—and the "gift" of whiskey and marijuana. I heard wheels turn on South Diego. I walked fast to a fence, over it, and across a littered backyard out into the next street. I heard no pursuit; my attacker's little frame-up hadn't worked. I'd get back to my car, change my clothes, and then find David Eigen again. If that had been Judy, she had not run from me on her own, no.

I walked in the direction of The Easy Dollar bar. The patrol car stopped across the street as I reached a corner. One of the policemen got out. I saw his alertness, his hand on his pistol. For a second I wondered who he was staring at. Then I knew.

"You!"

I took one step toward him to tell him who I was, show my— And I remembered. I had a gun, and no identification. I smelled of whiskey, and there would be traces of marijuana in my pocket. I turned and ran.

"You! Stop!"

I reached the first corner, with his feet pounding behind me. I ran across the street and into an alley. I went down the alley and over a high fence. I dropped down into a broken-down backyard, ran through it, and out across a second street. In another alley, I stopped and flattened against the wall, breathing hard. I heard whistles blowing near, the squeal of tires at some corner.

The two policemen who had stopped me that day near Pete Wallace's house came into my mind. They had called, "You!"—but then I had had the identification to change the "You" into "Sorry, *sir.*" Now I didn't, and in the alley, flat against a wall, whistles and growling police cars looking for me, I knew what it was in our land to be poor, or black, or brown, or even red, and in the wrong place—and what it was to be both at once. I suddenly felt how it was to live in the ghetto, and not be able to reach in my pocket and prove I was a man you said "Sir" to, a man who counted, who had position and status that demanded at least respect.

I could, eventually, prove who I was, and they would, of course, apologize, but I knew too well what could happen to me before then. I had seen it only a few days ago. No, that was only child's play, a few bad apples drugged with hate and gone hysterical, but not so hysterical they even then dared go too far in what they did. That wasn't a whole system geared to treat me as an animal, degrade me, assault me as a matter of course because I was no one, nothing, an enemy.

And what if I did not know at the back of my mind that in the end I could prove I was a person of status? What if, in this dark ghetto, I knew I had no status, and identification would not save me? Nothing would save me. If my face told them I was not a "Sir" and never could be? What if I flattened in this alley against the wall and knew that there was no help for me anywhere? No help but the hidden ghetto itself? Then . . .

"You! There!"

He was at the head of the alley. I ran again. To a fence, and . . .

The shot exploded behind me. "You, stop!"

. . . over the fence, flat down on my face. Up and running down another alley, plunging down into a doorway, through a dark cellar, up and out into the street. A squad car moved slowly in the distance. I ran on into more alleys, more garbage-strewn backyards, deeper into the ghetto. Really afraid now—afraid for my life.

I could be shot. I had run. No game, no theory here in this black ghetto. My life now; serious and coldly it was my life I could lose. I was running, and I was white, yes, but I was in the ghetto and the night was dark. I remembered Felicia Morgan's story—I could be shot down before they knew I had done anything at all. My life.

I scurried through alleys, backyards, deserted buildings, dank cellars, like a hunted rat looking for somewhere to rest. I was in the ghetto, and I was afraid. The final message, the ultimate truth—here I lived these moments as they, the citizens trapped here, lived every day of their lives. In fear. They would shoot now, the police. I had run too much, too far, and they did not know what I might have done. I might be a killer. I might be anything. I was guilty.

I was also in a ghetto, where my face did not belong. Here there was no safety for me. Black faces watched me, wary and hard. That I had not been stopped by a black face yet was a measure of their own scared lives—I was white, I had a gun in my hand now, and I could be a cop. Or maybe I was on the run, and they understood that— many of them. There were many others who understood only the law of ghettos—take care of yourself, grab anything you could.

I tried the streets again. I was deep in the ghetto now, like a prisoner escaped from Devil's Island. I kept moving, looked at the ragged buildings for some haven. Lighted or dark, the buildings here offered no refuge to me. For that, I was to blame as much as anyone else.

Someone moved behind me. Three black men, spread out and moving softly at me. I turned with my gun. They stopped, then seemed to melt away. They would be back, with friends. I ran.

A short white-haired man came out of a lighted candy store in front of me. Dressed in a neat black suit. I stopped him, my gun in his chest.

"Black Panther headquarters," I said. "Quick!"

"Mister, I ain't lookin' for no—"

"The Panthers, take me there!"

He was shaking, but he led me across three streets, then down two more long blocks. He pointed to a grimy three-story brick building. A sign above the basement door read: The Black Panther Party for Self-Defense. I let the old man go, and ran for the steps down. I hammered on the door.

"Pete! Pete Wallace! Morgan!"

The door opened. I fell inside, my gun still in my hand. Two young boys leveled shotguns at me.

"No!"

John Morgan stood at an open inner door. The shotguns lowered.

Morgan said, "Cops?"

"I lost them," I said. "A street gang, too."

I panted, still scared, but my mind raced—John Morgan wasn't missing any more.

39 ⌒

"Someone bumped you?" Morgan said. "At The Circle?"

We were in an inner room—John Morgan, Felicia Morgan, and three other men. Pete Wallace wasn't there. I sat in a chair, still breathing hard. It was a large room, full of desks, chairs, cots, and a pair of busy mimeograph machines. Posters of Huey P. Newton and Eldridge Cleaver hung on the walls. A rack of rifles and shotguns stood in a corner. At the rear was a locked steel door.

"You know The Circle people?" I said.

"I know them." He was behind his desk. "Most of them are kids who want to be left alone, but they're in a dream world. The Man'll blow them away, useless."

"A dream world like Judy Carlos'?" I said. "Who drives the yellow sports car there? Who leads them around, Morgan?"

Felicia Morgan said, "Back off, honky."

Her rhetoric knifed through my aching head. I leaned on the desk, my face close to Morgan. "Damn you all! Lies, silence, rhetoric! Judy's alive, but someone wants her dead! You think she's a spy. You lied all the way about her. Frank Carlos knew the men who tried to kill him—so they wore masks. It was a man and a woman who attacked my wife. Masked again. Why the masks for her? Maybe because black faces are noticed in Hollywood? You've been missing for two days, maybe more. If you've done anything to Judy, I'll see you all dead!"

The door opened behind me. I didn't turn. I knew that the two guards were there with their shotguns. Felicia Morgan's mouth curled in hate. The three men I could see sat rigid. Only John Morgan didn't react, his black face as quiet as Emil Tarra's old bandit eyes.

"Get the honky out, Papa," Felicia Morgan said. "Let his own pig cops cut him down."

I ignored her, faced only Morgan across the desk. "I'm sick, Morgan. Sick of you and the police using everyone. Sick of a war that maybe's trapped a girl who never hurt anyone except herself because she wants to give too much. I don't care about your war now. I loved that girl once, damn you!"

My neck crawled at the sounds behind me, the cocking of

shotgun hammers. But I faced John Morgan, and all at once I knew that he, too, faced only me. Between Morgan and me. His tragic face that could hide the world if it had to. A face that knew more than the other faces in that room. His soft voice was low.

"Where I've been is my business, Shaw, our business," he said. "Some things we keep for ourselves, we tell no one." He thought for a moment. "Okay, you want it all. Judy was here that night, yes. She left at nine o'clock, alone. None of us saw her again. All I know about that yellow car is that a lot of The Circle men drive it."

"What did she say that night? Where was she going?"

"She came to talk about Frank Carlos again. She said she wanted to do her work. She was going back to L.A. to work, and something about stopping a fake first, a lie. That's all."

"A fake? What fake? Someone, or something?"

"That's all, Shaw," he said, his face impassive.

"She's afraid, Morgan, running!"

"We're all running, all afraid," he said.

"To hell with your speeches! Nothing for one woman trying to give to the world, too?"

"No," he said, "nothing. I won't cry for her. She wants to hide from the fight. What happens to her is her own fault. Her apathy will destroy her. Look—" He reached into his desk, threw a folder out in front of me. "Read it."

There were four sheets in the folder. I read them. It was a detailed police plan of how to attack the headquarters. Here, where I stood. Machine guns, tear gas, assault squads, bullets to be fired down through the floor, provision for the dead to be carried away—Panther dead. All by surprise. I had seen such plans before. I pushed it away.

Morgan said, "One woman? One woman who wants to live apart, when my people face that every day of their lives? No, our goals are too important for one woman to matter."

"Goals?" I said. "What goals? Destruction? Killing?"

"The same goals you want, Shaw. A decent education, good jobs, homes without rats, life without fear. We feed poor kids breakfast, we register voters so that we can gain control of our lives. We want the same as King wanted, but we won't sing for it, we'll fight for it. We fight for the millions who don't count, the oppressed of the world."

His last words rang like a clarion call in the room. He lived his life now making speeches.

I said, "A man can use a fight for millions to hide a fight for one. A lot of crimes have been covered by manifestoes."

His face grew distant. "I guess that's so, Shaw."

I waited, but he didn't go on.

"Morgan," I said, "If you know—"

I became aware of a light flashing faintly on his desk. Felicia Morgan's voice was sharp: "Papa!"

The light was on the telephone. Morgan looked at the phone for a long few seconds, his face suddenly very tired. Then he picked up the receiver, listened. "Again? Okay."

He hung up, stood. "Another raid. Watcher just spotted them. They know I'm back. What do we have here now?"

"Nothing," one man said. "All clean."

"Plan Two, then. No shooting. I'll start on the bail when they go." He started to stuff papers into a case. The others moved quietly to posts.

"Why are they raiding again now?" I said.

He looked at me. "Why? Chase, harass, trap. Good trick, coming back so soon. Make us overreact. You ever think about the coincidence that *all* our top leaders are in jail, exile, or dead? For crimes, Shaw. Kind of bad odds, isn't it, that *all* of them would be caught in some real crime, a nonpolitical crime? Like saying all Jews in Germany were bank robbers."

"Can I get out of here?" I still had no identification.

"Scared?"

"Yes."

His dark eyes studied me. "Okay, come with me," he said, and looked at his wife. "Felicia, baby?"

"I'll stay, Papa. Pushing women makes them look bad."

They unlocked the steel door in the rear wall. Morgan went through, and I went behind him. I heard the screech of tires out in the street now, the slamming of car doors.

The steel door closed behind us. Morgan raised a trap door. We dropped down into a narrow passage under the floor.

40 ⌒

WE CAME OUT into a cellar. Morgan trotted across it and up into the street. A deserted street. The police were on the next block, and everyone knew that, and faded away.

Morgan crossed the street, went down an alley, across a second street, and into another building. He unlocked a door. We went into a small, bare room. He locked the door, put down his case, and sat on the floor against the wall. He didn't even look at me. He took out a cigarette, smoked.

I sat against another wall, facing him. His eyes stared straight ahead as he smoked. His tragic face was set, the muscle cords in his jaw standing out. He was more tense than I had ever seen him. Alone, all the quiet calm of command was gone. There were sudden shots in the distance. A few shots, about where the headquarters was. His face twitched at each shot.

I found a cigarette, lighted it. I smoked, wondering how I was to get out of here. It would be triply dangerous now—the police all around, the blacks angry. But I had to get back to that hidden pad of The Circle. I—

"You ever sit and wonder if that last shot maybe killed your wife, Shaw?"

"No," I said, "but my wife has been stabbed, and I sit and wonder if a girl I once loved is dead."

"Yeh," he said. His voice shook. "I hate violence!"

His tragic face was somber in the dark room. He smoked, flinched when there was another shot in the distance. His voice seemed to shiver.

"I've been in and out of jail since I was eighteen," he said. "Orphanage to jail, just like Pete Wallace, and most of us. Felicia got caught stealing when her mother was sick, and they couldn't stay alive on $148 a month from welfare. You know, nothing's more stupid than the idea we're 'becoming' two societies today—we were never anything except two societies. I went to prison first for rape. I was seventeen when it happened; the girl was fifteen, and it was her idea. Her folks said I sweet-talked her; the judge called it rape. What would have been juvenile delinquency for a white boy was rape for me. I was from the wrong society. Later I went up for assault. I almost killed a black storekeeper pulled a knife on me when I caught him cheating my kid sister. The judge didn't hear me."

He was nervous, afraid for his wife, talking to explain to himself what he was doing.

"I expect a police ambush every day. If I resist, I'm a law-breaker. If I don't, I'm maybe dead. In your world they'd look at who you are, and wonder why the police attacked you—the cops'd have to prove why they did it. In my world they'd look at who I am, and wonder what I'd done to be attacked, and I'd have to prove the police were wrong. Most white men have lost sight of their own ideals. You can't defend privilege, and still defend freedom. The ideals of this country are in the black, brown, poor, and young now. We're the only ones who remember that man was put here to make the world good for all men, not just for a few."

He was digging deep inside himself. I watched him. Why? His eyes seemed to be seeing that mountain he had to climb in his life, yet he was talking to me. To me, not to anyone else. Examining his life to tell me something he wanted me to know. Justifying some act? I let him talk, waited.

"We use violence to make speeches into reality. Sometimes we get violence we don't . . ." He stopped, smoked. "I've seen riots, men throwing Molotov cocktails and laughing to see the buildings burn; proud, feeling good inside. They feel reborn as men, doing something, fighting. That's a good feeling when you've been held down all your life. But it's wrong, no good. We can't just feel good, we've got to be intelligent enough to win." His tense face turned to me. "The real trouble is simple. Most white men just don't like black men, or brown men. Not economic, not political, just social. They don't like us, don't want us around, period."

"So then you reject all whites? Destroy them?"

All whites? Judy? A white woman who had become an enemy because she wanted to weaken the cause by removing a man they needed? An act to free Frank Carlos for the cause? Was that what Morgan wanted me to understand? Forgive?

"Not whites who have the same issues we do—a common enemy. When they know who the enemy is, we want them with us. We know we can't tear down the system just with guns. We need political action, too. But now we're in the phase of war, and people get hurt. Individual tragedy can't block the liberation of everyone."

"What individual tragedy, Morgan?"

"Any individual," he said. "We're trying to build social justice. If we took power and treated whites like they've treated us, I'd turn on my own people! If we don't learn, if we act like the whites, then we deserve to be crushed, too! I don't want your world, Shaw, I want a better world for both of us—our world! Black, white, brown—everyone."

I listened, watched his face. "What happened to the rhetoric? No pigs, no honkies, no violent names? You're talking now like a man who thinks. Why use the rhetoric at all?"

He didn't smile, but his face softened. "You know the yarn of the man asked to move a mule no one else could make move? He picked up a club and slammed the mule between the eyes. When they asked him why, he said, 'You got to get their attention first.' The rhetoric they remember, that's one reason."

"What's the other?"

"To make everyone realize that we're not the same as other civil-rights groups, that today's kids aren't just juvenile rebels like Dad was. We're different, we're serious, and we mean to win—all the way."

"Win? Against power, hate, and ten-to-one odds?"

"All revolutions start with a few men ready to die to make the majority see the truth," he said. "What chance did the Sons of Liberty have? What chance did the Russian socialists have in 1870? Read your history. Robert Emmett died in 1803, Irish freedom didn't come until 1922. I've studied the Irish fight because I think it's more like us than Lenin or Mao—a few militants for over a hundred years with no real base, either workers or peasants. Small and few they died for a hundred years, but when the majority finally saw the truth, the radicals were *there*, ready. Until 1916 ninety percent of the Irish tried to get free by negotiation. After 1916 they finally realized that no one lets slaves be free without a fight, and in six years ninety percent went over to the rebel view, and England was beaten."

"You're ready to wait a hundred years?"

"Is there another way?" Now I saw the fanatic in him, in that look toward the distant mountain of his goal. "We can't live as we are, Shaw. We know the system has failed, not from some theory of Marx's or anyone else, but from our own eyes. What white men can know only through theory, we know from our daily lives. The ethical society we want can't come from the system today. It hasn't worked except for the few, it can't be modified."

His cigarette had gone out long ago. He found another, lighted it, his face ravaged in the spurt of light. "For now, even if a man knows the strong will beat him, resistance at least makes him feel human, brings an inner peace no matter how futile. It's better to die for good than live for bad."

I said, "After 1922, and freedom, the Irish rebels turned around and fought each other like dogs over a bone. No peace."

"People make mistakes, and all fights attract opportunists," he said, his voice suddenly flat. "Sometimes we unknowingly do, or foster, acts we hate. The hurricane we release blows down bystanders. A backwash to every struggle, Shaw."

I heard it again in his voice, saw it in the way he sat against that wall. He was asking me to understand. What? "You know about Judy!" I said. "Something! Where is she? What do you know, Morgan?"

"I didn't say that," he said.

"What is it, Morgan? What's going on I—?"

"Hold it!" A gun appeared in his hand.

The door lock turned. Two Panthers came in, fast and quiet. One covered me with his gun, the other spoke to Morgan.

"They took them all. Felicia kicked up a boss storm," he said. "There's a cat outside wants to see you, Johnny."

Morgan said, "Drive Shaw to the border, shoo him out."

I said, "Morgan—"

He pointed a finger at me. "Walk away, Shaw. Now!"

They took me out to a car—a black sedan! I got in, and looked back. John Morgan stood alone in the street. As the car pulled away, I saw a massive shape appear next to Morgan. Perry Lint!

The bullet-headed private operator and Morgan stood alone. Perry Lint talked hard, and Morgan listened.

41 ~

THEY DROPPED ME near The Easy Dollar bar. They drove off without a word. I was irrelevant. Maybe I was.

I walked to my car, got in, and drove this time to South Diego Street. I parked at the rear of the condemned building where the yellow sports car had been. I went up those sagging stairs again. The door was open, and one lone candle burned in the room of mattresses and blanketed windows. No one was there, but I saw light through the door in the plywood partition.

I stepped to the opening. A man stood in the second room, near the left wall. No one else was there. The man held a gun and a candle, and was looking down. He hadn't heard me.

"Put the gun on the floor," I said.

I saw his back tense and stiffen.

"Don't do it," I said. "Put the gun down."

He laid the gun on the floor, and turned—Frank Carlos. I stepped to him. "Where've you been, Carlos?"

His voice was vague, like a man sleepwalking. He seemed to be trying to understand something. "Looking for her. I can't find her. I found him."

I picked up his pistol, and looked down to where he had been staring. It was a low old trunk. It was open. Max Alfreda was stuffed inside, still in his monk's robe. The stink of death was strong. I bent down. Alfreda's body was limp. He had been shot twice in the chest. Dead five or six days.

Frank Carlos said, "I looked for Elliot. I went to the cabin. I looked for Dave Eigen and Dr. Eyk. I couldn't find Eigen, and Dr. Eyk was home alone, drinking. He hadn't seen Judy, he said. He said John Morgan had maybe seen her last. I went to find Morgan. The cops were at Panther headquarters, so I came here."

I was looking at Max Alfreda in that trunk. In the end, had he been happy? At the last moment, had he welcomed his own vision of the insane violence at the core of human life, accepted the truth of dark disorder? What had killed him, a man who had lived only to give the world his vision of the truth? A mistake? A bystander blown down by the hurricane Morgan had talked about? I thought of John Morgan and his words, maybe his secret, and I thought about Scott Keating telling me he had talked to Alfreda, when Alfreda must have been already dead. Keating had lied, unless he had been the last to talk to Max Alfreda.

Frank Carlos said, "She never killed Alfreda. Not Judy."

"She said he was one of those trying to kill her," I said. When? When had she said it? After Alfreda was dead!

"I can't believe it," Carlos said. "All day there's been something, Shaw. In my mind. You told me about her, about seeing her, and I ran to find her, but—"

His voice was clearer, calmer, breaking out of the feel of a trance, maybe because I was there. He'd been alone all day, looking for Judy. I talked it out, told the whole story over again, from her first call to the darkness of Wilshire Boulevard: ". . . I was walking along just behind those three men. She came out of the doorway across Wilshire, waved to me, smiled, and . . ."

"Waved?" Carlos said, cried. "Smiled at you? You were close to three men, and she waved to you across Wilshire at night? She waved *first?*"

"That's right, and then—"

Carlos sat down on the floor, his legs collapsing. "You stupid idiot! You damned fool! That's what I've been hearing all day!" His head moved back and forth. "It wasn't Judy. No!"

I said, "I *saw* her, Carlos. You think I don't know—"

"Her glasses, damn you! She can't see across a street in daylight without her glasses. Not enough to pick you out!"

Her glasses. Six years. Judy never wore her glasses in public, had always been going to get contact lenses. The woman I had seen had not worn glasses, either. Six years.

"She never got contacts?" I said.

"Couldn't wear them," Frank Carlos said. "You just wanted to see her! You wanted it to be Judy so much you *saw* her."

I had *wanted* to see her, yes, that was it. Our brains are like that, yes. I had heard a soft voice, heard my memory of Judy's voice, and made the two into one. My memory of her voice had become the voice on the telephone, and once I had *heard* her, even with my doubts, my eyes then *saw* her easily—saw what they were eager to see, wanted to see.

"The woman must have looked a lot like Judy," Carlos said.

"A lot," I said, which, of course, is what had given them the idea. "All a setup. Neat. A girl like Judy, in Judy's clothes. One car drives up, acting menacing, and I react as I had to by shouting a warning. She runs, and another car is waiting to give her an escape. At least three people, and one a woman. They could have done it a hundred ways, depending on how I acted. A trick to muddy it up, accuse a man already dead, put doubts in my mind about you. The woman used the right words, wore Judy's clothes, and I saw what I wanted to see."

"Her clothes?" Carlos said. "Then . . . they must know where she is, they must have her somewhere, Shaw!"

Have her? Yes, but where? I looked around the silent pad of The Circle people.

I said, "Carlos, how did you happen to look for her here?"

"Here? I found this at the cabin, so I came."

He held out an Indian-style headband. The kind of band

worn today by long-haired men as well as women. It was painted with symbols, all variations of a circle.

"In the cabin? You were there before me, yes."

"It was mixed in the bed, I recognized it. The Circle kids. I had to ask where they were now. After I saw the cops at Panther headquarters, and split, I came here."

"Then," I said, "some of The Circle people were at the cabin. How? Only Judy and Emil Tarra knew where the cabin was. Dave Eigen knew it was Tarra's cabin, but not where it was. Unless he lied, and that doesn't matter. What matters is that only Judy or Tarra could tell anyone where the cabin was, so Judy must have told—"

Carlos said, "Judy must have taken them there, or—"

We both heard what he didn't say—or they took her there! I looked at the dead Max Alfreda, remembered Gloria Kazko.

"Come on," I said.

Max Alfreda had waited a week, almost, he could wait a few more hours. I had started on my own, I'd finish it on my own.

We went out to our cars. Carlos' gray VW was parked on the street. He followed me through the night city toward the Freeway to the mountains.

42 ᕫ

AN OWL HOOTED far off. Small things scurried in the brush. The snow crunched under our feet as we walked into the cabin on the point of land that jutted out into the pond. The vast Sierra night was brittle with the cold.

Inside the cabin it was colder than out in the night. I turned on the lights. Nothing had changed since the last time. Frank Carlos began to search, unaware of the cold. I knelt down over the blood I had found earlier. It was old, yes, maybe three weeks. No attempt had been made to clean it up. I stood, widened my search of the floor in slow circles. Something glinted near the rear door when I moved my head at a certain angle. I picked between the floor-boards. A tiny green button.

"Carlos," I said.

He came, took the button. "A row of them on her green dress sleeves. I used to ask her what the hell they were for."

"Easy, Frank," I said. "We know she was here."

"Her button?" he said. "Blood? The hairband I found in the bed?"

Carlos opened the rear door of the cabin, and we went out back. The snow had been trampled, partly by me earlier. There wasn't a lot of clear, or semi-clear, land between the cabin and the pond, and on both sides of the point the slopes were rocky with large boulders. Carlos saw the toolshed.

He had courage, Frank Carlos. He went straight to the shed. I walked behind him. Inside the small shed everything was neat. Two shovels and a pickaxe leaned against the wall. Dirt clung to all three tools. All right, up here you buried your garbage, your trash. There were a lot of reasons for digging. Frank Carlos took a shovel and the pickaxe. I took the second shovel. The ground would be hard, frozen.

We searched the point of land together. It would have been more efficient to separate, but somehow neither of us even mentioned that. We needed to be near each other in that cold mountain night. There was nothing but deep, un-broken snow until we reached the outer edge of the open area. There, on the left, between the pond and the first mas-sive rocks, we found two places where the earth had been dug, and only a few inches of new snow covered the fresh-turned dirt.

There was no need for the pickaxe, only the surface was frozen. Carlos took the left dug-spot; I took the right. We dug in silence. He dug faster, like a man hypnotized by some fear he wanted to run from but rushed toward instead. It didn't take long. The holes weren't very deep. In the end, Carlos was on his knees, digging eagerly with his hands in the dirt and snow. He held the flattened cans, the bread wrappers.

"Garbage," he said, and grinned up. "Trash!"

It was all I had found, too. Garbage and trash. Some grainy, frozen coffee grounds.

We both sat in the snow. I didn't grin. I was looking all around again in the night, the fingers of light from the cabin lying across the snow. The whole open space was under thick snow everywhere else. Except—

"Over there," I said, "behind the woodpile."

Carlos looked. The woodpile was undisturbed, but a few feet behind it there were three piles of brush that had been cleared from the edge of the open area to widen it. They were only lightly covered with snow, as if the wind kept them blown thin. I got up and walked to one of the piles to see if what I had noticed was so. It was. Some of the torn and cut brush ends were paler than the rest. The top layer, newly cut. Carlos stood beside me. He began to push the brush away, tumble it off the place it covered.

The dirt under the pile was soft, and there were few grubs or insects. We dug a wide hole over the uncovered spot. We both dug. Four feet down, Frank Carlos hit something. He scraped off the dirt for a few feet. It was soft and white, a shoulder. Carlos dropped his shovel. He walked to the line of boulders. He held onto the boulders with both hands, and vomited on his shoes.

I dug. My mind tried not to think, to think of nothing, only to dig as I had to dig until she was uncovered. It could be no one else. I dug, and fought to not think. I had to think, that is what our brains are for, and there is no way out. I thought: Judy . . . Oh, damn, damn, damn . . . I thought: It's over, Judy, no more. I thought: I'm not sick. Hollow, empty, but not sick. Frank Carlos was sick; she had been his woman. I thought, knew: If it was Maureen in this grave, I would be sick. I would be there at the rocks, vomiting, while another man uncovered the naked body of my wife. I thought: It's a lousy way to know that you loved your wife more than a memory, that your wife was the woman you wanted, needed.

I thought: Stop it, Paul! She's dead, and you knew all along that she was dead. Three weeks, and there was no way for her to be alive and silent. She's dead, gone. Now there was only her killer.

I crouched down over the hole. I tried not to look at her face. I had seen that face in darkened rooms, her hair across the pillow, her eyes wide up at me, and . . . stop!

I looked down at her. She was naked. She lay on her side. There were bruises on her back. She had been shot and stabbed. Slashed savagely, cut and hacked. Here, on this spot; there was not enough blood anywhere else. The left side of her head had been hit with some hard weapon, was matted with blood.

I stood up. I saw in my mind, out in the cold and snow, how she had died. A blow on the head, after the blows that had made the bruises. Hit on the head, and a wound that had bled in the cabin, but had not bled much. Half conscious, maybe, she had been dragged out here. No—there were no marks in the snow of dragging. She had been carried out here, into the cold and snow, and here, naked, she had been stabbed and shot. Here, at her grave, coldly and insanely stabbed and shot and slashed over and over. I could only hope that she had been dead long before the savagery ended.

I searched that grave, and her naked body so cold when

I remembered its warmth. I had to search that grave, look for any clue. I found nothing. I walked to the rocks. Frank Carlos still leaned against the boulder, his head down, but no longer vomiting. Dry, racking spasms in his throat and chest. I sat on a rock. I found a cigarette, lighted it. I smoked in the cold and silent mountain night.

She was dead. The end of all her new days; today and eternity gone. No more eagerness for the new day that was going to be her day, a better today than yesterday had been, the yesterday that never existed for her. Nothing had ever been what she wanted, what she struggled to find in herself and in the world. Nothing. Now she had tried once more to have what she wanted—her art and Frank Carlos working for a vision—and had lost it all.

No, not lost it, had it taken from her. A gentle girl who had always faced her own truths, no matter what they were. Who had never learned to hide what she felt or thought— and was that what had killed her? Yes, I was sure of that. The savagery of her death. Who had she told a truth that maddened? What had she done, openly, that had driven someone to murder?

Frank Carlos moved, pushed himself away from the rock, looked toward the opened grave. His scarred and pitted face was very calm. The pain there only in the whiteness of the pits and scars on his brown, faintly Indian face.

"When, Shaw?"

"That Tuesday night, I think," I said. "She wasn't seen after nine o'clock that night. She was planning to go back to L.A., hoped to come here with you. Sometime after nine o'clock that night. She told John Morgan she had to stop a fake first, stop a lie. She'd talked to Elliot about pigs, the slimy underbelly of virtue."

"A pig? A fake? Then—"

"Unless they were lying, one or both of them," I said.

He stared at the grave across the snow. "Where do we go, then? Do we ever find out, Shaw? How?"

"In time we'd have to find out, a killer like that," I said. "They can't hide forever, not anyone who would kill like that."

"In time? Yes, maybe," he said.

I said, "There's one place, one man. Scott Keating. He keeps changing his story of what he's doing, what he is. It never figured, really, that he'd be involved with Max Alfreda. He may have lied about Alfreda, knew Alfreda was dead. Or guessed. He's mixed all through this, and I don't think we know why, not really. He's weak, maybe the weak link."

Frank Carlos began to walk. He didn't look at the grave as he passed. I did. She, too, like Max Alfreda, could wait a little longer for police and cameras and autopsy, for the indifferent hands on her. But there were animals in these mountains, and I stopped to cover her up again.

I was sweating in the cold when I finished and walked through the cabin, turning off the lights. In front, Frank Carlos waited in his car for me to drive out first.

43 ⌒

No CARS STOOD in the drive of the big, old frame house a mile before Nugget, but there was light in a rear window upstairs. There was no other light. We drove into the semi-shabby yard this time, and Frank Carlos followed me up the porch steps to the front door. No one answered our ring.

I tried the front door. It was locked. I used my keys. The second one opened it—an old lock. Inside, the fine old furniture gleamed quietly in the darkness. It was very late

now, little traffic on the county highway outside. We made
noise as we walked around the downstairs, but no one called
from the lighted room above. Maybe Keating, or someone,
slept with a light on. We went up.

The door of the lighted room stood ajar. It was at the end
of a long upstairs hall. I motioned Frank Carlos back, and
pushed the door open. The room was clean and Spartan.
Hand-hewn furniture on a bare floor that gave a sense of
space. A pitcher stood in a washbowl on a homemade side-
board with leather hinges on the cupboard doors. The bed
was iron and narrow, covered only with a blanket. Rifles
hung on the walls, and nothing else. It was like a frontier
room from the last century. A pioneer room where a man
lived alone.

A thin, old man sat in a crude rocker at the window. He
wore a stained brown sombrero on his thin white hair, a
heavy wool shirt, and faded whipcord trousers that flapped
loose around his legs. His feet were in slippers; a pair of
work boots stood on the floor next to the narrow iron bed.
His face was shrunken and like dry leather, and his eyes,
sunk in deep creases, were clear blue as he turned to look at
me.

"Who are you, son?"

"Paul Shaw," I said. What had Keating said? That his
father lived here. "Mr. Keating?"

"I don't know you."

"I came to find your son."

"Scott? He left."

The old man swung back to the window. His legs were
stiff, feet flat on the floor. He moved the chair with his arms
only, his shoulders big for his size, but all bone under the
shirt now. Frank Carlos stood behind me, started to walk
past me toward the old man. I stopped him. The old man
was watching out the window again. The mountains would
have been clear and close in daylight. In the night they
were a heavy shadow.

"Light up on Saddleback. Someone up there," the old man said, his gaze up toward the tiny point of light. "Not much to see now, but I don't sleep so well, and it's dawn in a few hours. My day woman doesn't come before eight. Can't stand women around after that wife of mine. She had the money that ruined Scott. You have to spend money. On yourself if you want, or on others, but use it. The trouble today is that we hoard money. Having it, keeping it, is more important than using it."

"Where is Scott, Mr. Keating?" I said.

"My name's Jason. I don't know. He lives in Pasadena. I never go there. He's got a wife like his mother. I outlived my wife and her money, but it doesn't do me much good. My legs won't work. I sit in a box as deep as Scott's."

"Mr. Keating!" Frank Carlos said. "We have to find—"

The old man turned. "Scott's mixed in trouble. I know."

"What trouble?" I said.

Jason Keating heard his own voices. "I don't like the way my son lives, or how he thinks. I'm eighty-two. I was sixteen when I came West. Scott hates the kids today. I don't. Where do they go to escape what they don't like or want? I had open land to find, nature to fight. They have no escape, and nothing to fight but dry old men."

He looked at me, and at Frank Carlos. "Scott doesn't tell me much, but I know he's hiding something. That's his way. Cover up, evade with money, never face anything straight. His mother and her money taught him and bought him. He uses his money to evade everything, even living."

"Some crime, Mr. Keating?" I said.

"Crime?" He blinked at us. "Angles and advantages, bought and paid for. That big black buck's mixed in it. Bad type."

"Perry Lint?"

He turned again to stare out at the night. "I knew the boy would bring him down someday. A boy is a fact, and you can't change facts with all the money there is."

"Boy?" I said. "What boy?"

The old man's head was down, his bent neck vulnerable. "He turned away, as if the boy didn't exist. How could anyone do that? All these years, I still don't know. He had a chance to be a free man, Scott did, and he lost it. He thinks he has the good life, when he has no life. Just comfort. He never even had another child, not one. Justice, maybe."

"Scott abandoned a son?" I said. "Can you tell us about it?"

Jason Keating nodded, faced us. "Twenty or twenty-five years ago now, my memory doesn't work too well. Scott ran away when he was eighteen. His mother found him living in a slum with a girl, working with radicals, trying to write about the poor. He already had the baby son, was going to marry the girl, work in the slum. I was away in Alaska. His mother brought him home, but it wasn't all her. She only found him because he'd made it easy; I think he wanted to run home then. All she had to do was show him the hard and the easy. He took the easy. I never saw the girl, or my grandson."

"Now the son's come back?" I said. "What's his name?"

"They called him young Scott then. I don't expect he kept the name. Scott was using a false name."

"When did he come back?"

"During the strike at the college, a year ago. Scott came here, pale as a ghost. I knew. Scott wouldn't talk about it, not much. Seems the boy knocked around all over. New York, Hollywood, making a living."

I said, "Do the names David Eigen or Rick Elliot mean anything to you?"

"No."

"What did the son want?"

"Money, I suppose," the old man said, and stopped. His blue eyes were deep in his leathery creases. "No, I don't know that, not at first. I think he only wanted a kind of revenge, to make Scott squirm, suffer. Scott gave him money

—what else would my son do for my grandson but pay him money? But I don't think the boy wanted money at first. Later, now, I think the boy's in some trouble, and Scott's helping cover it up."

"How did the boy find Scott?"

"I don't know," the old man said. "I know it wouldn't have been easy, and Scott would do anything to hide the boy, keep him away."

"Why?" I said. "Just because Scott would look bad for having abandoned the boy a long time ago?"

"Because he'd look bad in his world for ever having known the boy's mother," the old man said. "You see, that girl Scott lived with then was a black girl."

Frank Carlos' face jerked as if slapped. I don't know what my face was like, I didn't think about it, because at that instant it all fell into place. The key to the killings, the beatings, the attack on Maureen—especially the attack on Maureen.

In one moment I had the tie between Scott Keating, and Judy, and Max Alfreda, and all the others. I saw the key I had missed—the attack on Maureen.

44 ❧

THE SHABBY HOUSE at the end of Fremont Street was lighted. Light in all the windows even as dawn grayed the sky over the high mountains, and cast a faint morning chill over the debris-filled quarry. There were voices, and three cars were in the yard: Pete Wallace's old Chevy wagon, the yellow sports car, and the big black sedan I'd seen twice before.

Frank Carlos and I had our guns out. We stepped softly to a front window. As I looked into the lighted living room, the whole long week fell away—I saw the broad, muscular, long-haired young man who had driven the yellow sports car away from Carlos' road that first day. He wore a wool poncho now, and he sat on a couch—not alone. Beside him were two women. The older, painted girl from The Circle pad, and a younger girl I'd never seen but had seen—small, round, dark-haired: the girl who had been Judy!

Frank Carlos whispered, "Felicia Morgan!"

She stood in the room, facing the three on the couch. She had a pistol. Another Panther was with her. He had a gun, too. They were all silent, the voices coming from the other room.

I touched Frank Carlos. "I'll take Felicia."

The front door was ajar. I pushed it open quickly. Only the painted woman saw us, blinked vaguely. The others were listening to the voices inside. I touched my gun to Felicia Morgan's back.

"Be quiet. Hand me the gun, butt first."

I had her gun. Frank Carlos had the other gun. We sent Felicia and the other Panther to stand beside the three on the couch. Felicia's eyes hated me, but she said nothing.

"Keep them still, Frank," I said.

I stood in the doorway of the inner room. John Morgan had his back to the door. He had a gun. Pete Wallace was in a corner next to the bureau, backed into the narrow space between the walls and the bureau as if trying to hide. But he wasn't scared. His dark glasses were off, and his eyes were bright and defiant. He was watching only Morgan, and didn't see me.

Scott Keating did see me. The big, handsome man was flat against the far wall, between Pete Wallace and Mor-

gan, trying to vanish through the wall somehow. His terrified eyes rolled when he saw me. I took a step inside.

"Gun on the table, Morgan," I said. "We have Felicia."

Pete Wallace saw me. "Paul! Man, you look good!"

John Morgan laid his pistol on the table.

"You want to tell me now about Judy?" I said to Morgan. "About Perry Lint, and The Circle, and a fake?"

Morgan's ravaged face was grim. "She asked us to let
Frank Carlos quit. She went away; then there was the first
raid. She'd seen some automatic rifles and grenades, and
the cops knew all about those when they raided. Then Carlos called, said Judy was missing. What do we think, Shaw?
We looked around, talked to Dave Eigen. No one had seen
her. Then the cops come and tell us someone tried to kill
Frank Carlos. You came, still looking for Judy. What do we
think? Maybe she's changed sides against Carlos and us. So
we look some more, and we watch you, Shaw. I had the
brothers follow you down in L.A., and up here."

"The black car," I said. "It was tailing me."

Morgan looked at Keating. "You led us to Keating. We
checked on him and found who he is. Then we spotted you
tail Perry Lint to Keating. Lint is a piece of garbage, he'll
sell anything to anyone, but he doesn't know about us. So
who's giving him the scene for the police? I talked to him.
He knows his payoff is over, so he tells—Keating gave him
the info about us! He didn't tell Keating, Keating told him.
Tonight you told us about The Circle, and we know now
what goes."

I said, "And I know who killed Judy, and the others."

Scott Keating jerked like a spastic, muscles jumping his
arms against the wall. "Shaw, I've got money! I swear—"

I said, "You can't hide it any more, Keating," and I said
to John Morgan, "You came to get him?"

"We want him," Morgan said. "No one to know, Shaw."

"I'm sorry," I said. "I want him. Carlos wants him."

As we battled with our eyes, Morgan and I, the sound

came from the corner where Pete Wallace stood. A low, menacing hiss. The throat-hissing of a cornered animal. Pete's voice, through the low hissing, was light, pleasant.

"Hey, cats, what you two talking about? Clue me in."

Morgan said, "We've never been sure of him. He was too on his own, out for himself too much. Too quiet sometimes, too loud other times. Smooth and easy with the women, very nice. Felicia never believed him, said he was funny with women, just scalps to him, feed him."

The echo rang in my head—the same words Pete Wallace had used to describe Morgan and Dave Eigen. A clever, mocking game. Arrogant, using his own symptoms and hang-ups to describe his enemies. Clever, laughing at me, at everyone, all the time.

"The boy's smile," I said. "The innocent eyes."

The hiss from Pete Wallace's corner never stopped. As if it couldn't stop, like the automatic reflex of a cat's purr. A savage cat, unaware that he was making the sound, smiling.

"Hey, he's crazy, Paul. You know me. I'm helping you, right? I'll take over, okay?"

I said, "They'll all turn on you, Pete, the jackals you live with. You taught them. Your killings, assaults aren't the kind you can hide once it's opened up. You'll have left a trail of evidence, we've already got a headband. Keating'll talk. That money the first day at Max Alfreda's theater was really for you, right? To pay you to go far away. I can hear it all now, I understand what was happening. You didn't run, of course not, and the rest was all you and your pack trying to cover. Keating faces an assault charge on me, and accessory for covering for you. His lawyer'll make him talk. The only hold you had on him was fear. That's the only real hold you have on anyone."

Scott Keating said, "I . . . he's insane . . . My son . . . but . . ."

"What was it, Pete?" I said. "She said the plays you gave her were rotten, she wouldn't show them? Did you try to rape her? She wouldn't touch a man she didn't like, and she didn't scare, not Judy. Or did she know you were selling out the Panthers, had found out?"

The hissing from deep in his throat began to chill my spine. A sound he couldn't control any more than an animal could. A hissing from deep down inside where his small monster crouched. Still smiling, boyish, through the hissing rattle.

"Paul, you're crazy. I mean it. Really, man."

"No, Pete," I said. "You made one big mistake I should have seen earlier. Maureen was attacked. She and I hadn't been seen together once out here. Maureen is well known, but no one knows her husband except friends—and someone who knew us from the old days! Rick Elliot and you, and Judy might have told Carlos. Elliot and Carlos are clear. That leaves you."

His animal hissing sound stopped, the way it does when the animal is about to attack. He stood away from that corner, fixed us all with his eyes as if he were about to sweep us all aside by the power of his will, by his magnificent force.

His eyes glittered. "She came here, told me my plays stank! She wouldn't show them. The bitch female, jealous of my work! I know what to do with females. They like it hard, rough, on their backs. All of us on that bed—me, Yancy, the girls, Judy. I had to hit her, you know? She spit on me. I hit her harder with the gun. She'd told me before about that cabin she was gonna take Carlos to. I got the flash—all of us out there, a three-day bang, beautiful. Out there she'd come around. Only we get there, she don't come around, even when the girls talk to her, work on her. So I knocked her around to relax her, see? She says I'm crazy, a fake, a fink! Christ, I got tired of her. I killed her. I'm a man, see? We all carried her out in the snow, and I killed the bitch."

I was paralyzed. Scott Keating had turned to face the wall, beat his head against the wall. John Morgan walked to Pete, hit him once, twice, in the face. Pete fell to the floor. Morgan hit him again, hard. Pete lay still. I went to the telephone and called Lieutenant Devine. I just told him to bring his homicide crew.

I sat down to wait. John Morgan stood over me.

"Wallace was three when his mother ran out, too," Morgan said. "A cousin brought him up until he was ten. She died. Seven years he lived in alleys off what he could steal. In and out of reform schools. He knifed a guy in a fight, and ran to New York—to be an actor. He stole all the time to get money to live. No chance of a job—no training, no background."

I said, "Frank Carlos got out of the slum, Morgan."

"Most slum kids don't have Carlos' brains or talent. You don't build a society for the exceptional few," Morgan said. "Wallace had no talent. He drifted out of New York, got picked up in L.A. on robbery, paroled in two years. He got a way with weak women, he found The Circle to mix with. Another time he'd have been back in prison fast, but today, in the violence, he could blend in and hide. He found us. My record's as bad as his, maybe worse. We didn't know what he was inside. He's a mad dog, but I understand him. He might have gone crazy anywhere, any time—but do we know?"

"You'll mourn for him?"

"For the waste. For what help could have done for him."

"Okay," I said. "But mourn for Judy, too. And the others."

His tragic face was rigid. "Some good get hurt so everyone can be better. We want a world that doesn't make Pete Wallaces, or if it does, it doesn't abandon them."

We both listened in silence to the distant wail of sirens coming closer. Morgan said, "If they find us here, Shaw, they'll make this a weapon. He'll talk, but if we're not found here, we can disown him."

"Go," I said. "Tell Carlos I said so."

I sat alone.

Scott Keating sat on the bed. "Can I leave, Shaw?"

"You can't evade it now, no."

"I'll be ruined, destroyed."

"A bruise, no more. You can protect yourself."

"Not against my friends, even my wife." He shook his handsome head. "Almost twenty-nine years ago. I was eighteen. We . . . had a good year." His pale eyes remembered—a black girl he could actually have loved long ago, or the boy he had been. "The boy was born. I felt trapped, scared. I wanted my life, my—"

"Advantages," I said.

"Yes, of course," he said. "I'd used a false name with the girl, there was no trouble. We moved to Pasadena. I didn't come back to San Perdido for fifteen years. My father hates me. So did . . . Pete."

"How did he find you?"

"I spoke at an anti-strike meeting last year. Some old woman knew my face and voice. You can't bury all the past; there was a trail. Pete checked the birth records, found where we'd lived and others who'd known me. I'd spoken of my school, and he tracked down my real name through school pictures and records. He's clever, and he found me."

"He wanted money?"

"Not at first. What he wanted was to hate me to my face. He took money when he found out I headed our group of property owners, and decided to feed me facts against the Panthers." Keating looked around the decrepit room. "I don't know what he did with the money. It wasn't much—until he told me he'd killed that girl. Then I gave him five thousand dollars to get out of the country, to get far away from me!"

"You had no real connection to Max Alfreda at all, did you? You were at the theater that day to give Pete his money. I can hear it in my head. It was Pete who pretended you were a backer of Alfreda, Pete who told you to give the money to Alfreda so I wouldn't know what was really happening. You knew I was a detective, and you were scared. Alfreda went along with it."

Keating nodded. "I'd never met Alfreda before that day. I just followed Pete's lead. Later I made up more lies. All lies. Perry Lint didn't give me information, I gave it to him —from Pete. Pete couldn't let Lint know it was Pete arranging the raids on the Panthers. I think he hoped to discredit John Morgan and take over. His insane schemes!"

I remembered the afternoon I trailed Perry Lint to Keating. I'd had Keating scared—until I tried to trick him by saying that Pete Wallace had told me he knew Judy. After that he hadn't been scared—he knew it was a lie about Pete, because he and Pete were together in the affair all the way.

"You couldn't expose Pete, could you? Not even after he told you he'd killed Judy. No matter who else was killed!"

He cringed. "How could I let anyone know I was the father of Pete Wallace? In my world, my position? No! Then he killed that woman. The father of a black murderer! No one could ever know that. I paid him to run, and I sent Perry Lint to stop you before you found out. But Pete wouldn't go. He stayed!"

The sirens growled closer. Keating's eyes pleaded—let him evade one more time.

"I don't know who's more insane," I said. "You, or—"

I saw the movement too late. Pete Wallace was up. On his feet with a gun. A gun he must have had in some cunning hiding place for just such a moment. His violent eyes were glazed. He stepped to Scott Keating, took his arm.

"I'm going out of here," he croaked. "Don't chase me."

"No chance, Pete," I said.

He laughed. "I got money and a gun. What else do I need?"

He pushed Keating to a rear door. They went out as the sirens slowed at the corner of the street. I jumped to the window, my gun ready. In the dawn light I had no shot. Pete Wallace had Keating between us. He dragged Keating toward the deep quarry. If he reached the quarry, he might . . .

Frank Carlos came around the front of the house behind Pete Wallace. Pete heard him, and turned with his gun aimed. Carlos shot him four times. Pete's body jerked as all four shots hit. He fell on his back in the dawn. I ran out.

The hissing sound rose from Pete's throat, and then changed to a dry rattle as the light died from his eyes. The last look I saw in his dying eyes was one of pure hate.

45 ᕙ

It was past noon before Lieutenant Devine had it all enough in hand to sit down in his office with me. A sunny day, the streets of San Perdido alive and busy. In the office it was all unreal to me. Devine sat in his desk chair.

"The D.A. says justifiable homicide for Carlos: self-defense," Devine said. "Full inquest, though. With Carlos' name up here, the strike and all, the D.A. wants it all open. All kinds of trials. Maybe in three counties. Go on for years."

"But Frank Carlos gets off?" I said.

"On the shooting, yes. But he'll go back inside for a while. Parole violation. No way out. With his strike record, the good citizens'll want blood."

"They'll get blood," I said.

"Yeh," Devine said. "We've got all the bodies; we're filling in L.A. on Carlos being attacked. Everyone wants the details, but I'll cover your part, you solved it. The two girls are talking. The young one's scared, and the painted one doesn't give a damn. All the blame on Wallace and the other guy, the one who drove the yellow sports car. His name's Yancy, he was Wallace's pal in The Circle group, and he blames it on Wallace."

"They're crazy," I said, "but not all the way."

Devine shook his head. "They acted crazy enough. They buried Judy Carlos, figured they were safe—no one could catch them. Then Frank Carlos started calling around, and Wallace panicked. Crazy, you know? First too sure they're safe, then too quick to panic. Carlos knew nothing, but Wallace got scared. He came down to watch Carlos, and heard him hire you. So he got Yancy, put on the masks, and tried to kill Carlos. Only Frank Carlos is no girl. He fought them off, got his gun, and they ran. Two of them just ran. Irrational, you know? Arrogant one minute, rabbits the next. They talked up some Dutch courage—it took hours, and that's typical of nuts, too—and sent Yancy back in the yellow sports car to see how Carlos was. That's when you showed up."

"I spotted Yancy on the road. Stupid to let me see him."

The sun was hot through the windows. Devine nodded. "It was all stupid. Yancy ran to tell Pete he'd seen you going to Carlos, and that's when Pete went to Max Alfreda's place to meet Scott Keating and get the money Keating offered if he'd blow. But after Pete talked to you, he figured to fool you. He remembered the Kazko girl. She'd seen him with Judy, and she might know about the cabin. Just *might* know, but he and Yancy killed her anyway! It was fun, they were fooling you. Your wife was the same thing: smart pressure on you. And Wallace started worrying about Max Alfreda. God, he just had to tell what he'd done."

"A compulsion, Devine," I said.

"What I don't get is why Alfreda kept quiet. Keating, yes, he'd cover for Wallace, but why would Alfreda?"

"He was like a scientist," I said. "He was interested in the process of insanity, not in its results. He thought he could save the world by studying insanity. What were a few deaths if he learned to understand the world?"

Devine shook his head. "He didn't save himself. When he ran from you he joined Wallace. But you'd gotten too close to the truth in that theater, so Wallace killed Alfreda to shut him up. He had the body in that trunk for days—he forgot about it! They're like that, schizoids. They get lost in their clever plans. Know what they did with Judy Carlos' car? Sold it. Know what they did with all the money Wallace got? They were building an arsenal—armored jeeps, bombs! For his gang of nuts inside The Circle. Predators, Shaw, against all sides. They figured to live off everyone, keep the trouble boiling."

"What about David Eigen? Not involved at all?"

"He knew Wallace, and he'd sort of guessed. But he was too scared, he didn't want to get involved."

"What happens to Keating and Perry Lint?"

"Keating's lawyers are already working on the accessory charge here. L.A.'ll handle the assault on you. Perry Lint's on the run. We'll get him, but he didn't know anything."

Keating would have to defend Perry Lint to defend himself. There was only my word on the attack; good lawyers would get them both off. I didn't want to think about it.

"Can I talk to Frank Carlos?" I said.

"Sure," Devine said.

We went along the wide, cool corridors of the courthouse. It was a beautiful building—a Moorish castle from Spain. The citizens were proud of how it looked outside, a show-piece to impress visitors. Few of them knew what went on inside, if they ever even thought about that.

Frank Carlos sat in a cell. A dangerous parole violator.

He wasn't alone. Dr. Jonas Eyk stood up as Devine and I came in. He didn't look happy.

"Remember, Frank, if I can do anything," Eyk said to Carlos. "I . . . I felt very close to Judy."

"Try teaching the truth, Professor," Frank Carlos said.

Eyk winced as if slapped. "Yes. I'm afraid I failed all around—as a teacher and as a man. A poor father substitute."

He left without speaking to us.

Frank Carlos looked at Lieutenant Devine. "Will I get to tell my story, Lieutenant?"

"At your hearing and at the other trials. You'll be a witness. You want to tell it all? A tactic in a war?"

"I want to tell it all," Frank Carlos said.

"Then what, Frank?" I said.

"I go back to finish my sentence, what else?"

"After that?"

The pits and scars stood out on his drawn face, the oriental eyes were haggard. "She wanted us to sing in our art. The pure truth and eternal man. But she's dead, and it's too late to sing, or too early. Too late for her, too early for us all."

"Wallace was insane, Frank," I said.

"A rat," Frank Carlos said. "But we know that rats come from ruins, dirt, abandoned places. In a way he did me a favor. What Lenin said always preyed on my mind—you have to break eggs to make an omelet. I used to wonder if I'd be a broken egg, but it's Judy who got broken. I've got no more to lose. She got caught in the fight, and at least I can work to see that the right omelet gets made."

"Would she have wanted her death to mean that? She wanted you to quit the Panthers, not join them."

"She's gone!" he cried, glared. "You think I can sit and write plays? Camus said it—artists have to be men, too, even to the point of giving up your special calling to involve yourself. I want to end it, one way or the other. Judy's life was a child's dream that never came true. I want a world where it would have come true."

Devine said, quietly, "So do I, Carlos. Is violence the only way?"

Frank Carlos didn't seem to hear, he heard the voice in his mind. "A child's dream is true life. A child is real, himself. The world we call mature takes the vast, universal dreams of childhood and reduces them to small, manageable, irrelevant dreams of success in a false box. What we call mature adulthood is a false face we make of ourselves to please the outside world. Judy never made that reduction. She and Pete Wallace were the same. Wallace couldn't settle for a false face, and went insane. Judy refused to settle for a false face, and was killed. She maddened Pete because she didn't react like all the mature people he charmed, conned, or scared."

"So you abandon your dream too?"

"Maybe my dream is a sane world where no one kills, no one hates, no one has bombs, no one lives off others."

"You'll go with the Panthers?"

"When I get out of jail—if I get out."

Lieutenant Devine said, "Where do Shaw and I go, Carlos? We know how much is rotten, but we don't want war. Back in history a man of good will who didn't want to fight for any side went to a monastery. There aren't any monasteries now. Which side will take us or trust us? A man who wants change without blood? A cop who wants real justice?"

Frank Carlos shrugged. "I guess you'll just have to decide where you stand the most."

"Where does it all leave Judy, Frank?" I said.

"Dead, Shaw. It leaves Judy dead."

I said, "Good luck, Frank."

"Shaw?" he said. "Thanks. And send me a bill. I'll pay."

I left the cell, and I left the courthouse. They'd need me, but not for a while. The legal wheels would grind slow. The three Circle people would go to prison or mental hospitals, Scott Keating would get off with no more than a slap. Rick Elliot would explain what he'd been doing, it didn't matter much. He hadn't been involved, really, and he would spend his life explaining himself—to himself and to his wife.

David Eigen would probably end in political office—or, given these days, in jail. Dr. Jonas Eyk would go on trying to teach, wondering if what he taught had any real relevance. No one would bother Emil Tarra.

I drove out of San Perdido. I needed a few days on some beach with Maureen. She would be gentle to me while I lay in the sun and thought about Judy. I remembered when I had told Judy that I couldn't be part of her life—*"I'm glad, Paul, in a way. I want you, but I want my work too much to keep you. I don't ever want to hurt you, and I can't compromise."*

The sun was hot as I drove, the sky blue, and I thought of the violence that had killed Judy in its wake. I knew which side I was on, but that would not change much. I would make no more difference than Judy had. History would decide. Not me, and not the Nixons, or Reagans, or Ho Chi Minhs, or Castros, or John Morgans. History, and the millions of unknown faces across the whole world, would decide in the end who won.

History didn't care about the good people who died between the forces that struggled for the future; the small people slapped aside without malice or love, with a kind of indifference. History didn't care about the Pete Wallaces it created, or the Judys it killed. But I cared.

There had to be someone to cry for the innocent caught by chance and history, the flowers trampled under violent feet.

I cried.

About the Author

MARK SADLER writes of the rough side of our smooth world, of the criminal hidden under the "normal" surface. The son of a revolutionary politician turned actor, he has lived in New York, Los Angeles, Denver, San Francisco, upstate New York, Chicago, Canada, London, Paris, and other cities too numerous to mention. Educated, with a B.A. and an M.A., through four colleges, he has been an actor, stage-hand, farm worker, business editor, chemist, teacher, junior executive—and for twenty years a writer about the people and forces that shape our time. He has fought as an infantry soldier, lived in five countries, worked in stockroom and executive suite, observed at first-hand what makes men act for good or evil. Now he has set up his permanent home in Santa Barbara, where he writes of the dark despair and violence behind all the eager faces.